MW00955116

One Night In London

Sandi Lynn

Sandi Lynn

One Night In London

Copyright © 2016 Sandi Lynn

All rights reserved. No part of this publication may be reproduced, distributed, or transmitted in any form or by any means, including photocopying, recording, or other electronic or mechanical methods without the prior written permission of the publisher.

This is a work of fiction. Names, characters, places and incidents are the products of the author's imagination or are used factitiously. Any resemblance to actual events, locales, or persons, living or dead, is entirely coincidental.

Photo & Cover Design by: Sara Eirew @ Sara Eirew Photography

Models: Matthieu Grondin & Pamela Brisson

Editing by B.Z. Hercules

Books by Sandi Lynn

If you haven't already done so, please check out my other books. They are filled with heartwarming love stories, some with millionaires, and some with just regular everyday people who find love when they least expect it.

Millionaires:

The Forever Series (Forever Black, Forever You, Forever Us, Being Julia, Collin, A Forever Family)

Love, Lust & A Millionaire (Wyatt Brothers, Book 1)

Love, Lust & Liam (Wyatt Brothers, Book 2)

His Proposed Deal

Lie Next To Me (A Millionaire's Love, Book 1)

When I Lie with You (A Millionaire's Love, Book 2)

A Love Called Simon

Then You Happened

The Seduction of Alex Parker

Something About Lorelei

Second Chance Love:

Remembering You

She Writes Love

Love In Between (Love Series, Book 1)

The Upside of Love (Love Series, Book 2)

Table of Contents

Prologue

I nervously rummaged through my closet, trying to find my Louboutin black stiletto heels— shoes that were half off and then another seventy-five percent off the half-off price. They were a freaking steal and the only pair that was left happened to be my size. I stumbled upon them by accident, earlier in the week, when I was looking at the clearance rack, trying to find the perfect pair of shoes for my date tonight with Corey. He was taking me to my favorite restaurant because he had something he needed to discuss with me. It was no surprise, though. I already had my suspicions. He was going to ask me to move in with him.

Corey and I had been dating for almost nine months. We met when he and his mom came into the art gallery where I worked, looking for a painting for her bedroom. We got to talking, and he asked me out for coffee the next day. At first, I didn't think he was really my type, but then again, I never really knew what my type was. We had so much in common that it wasn't hard to fall for him. Corey, by far, had been the longest relationship I'd ever been in and he was a really nice guy. The only thing that bothered me was that he wasn't very sexual. Once every other week was more than enough for him and it was usually over with before it started. But I overlooked that problem because we always had so much fun when we were together. We loved the same movies, the same music, and he loved art almost as much as I did. We were perfect for each other and I knew the time was right to move in together. Although we never talked about it, I sensed it was what he planned to ask me. You're probably sitting there thinking that he's going to propose. That was off the table because neither one of us wanted to get married until we were at least a couple years older. Being twenty-four, we both felt we needed to be completely established in our careers before making a lifelong commitment.

I stood in front of my full-length mirror as I slipped into my heels and ran my hands down the sides of my short black dress with the V-neckline and three-quarter-length sleeves, which I also picked up on sale. Running my fingers through my long blonde hair, I lightly sprayed the curled ends, grabbed my purse, and headed to Sur in West Hollywood.

When I arrived, Corey was already seated and waiting for me. Butterflies fluttered around my belly at the thought of us moving in together. As I approached the table, Corey stood up and kissed my cheek. He was always such a gentleman.

"Hey. You look beautiful. I love that dress. Is it new?"

"Yeah. I bought it earlier this week along with these babies." I smiled as I stuck my foot out.

"Are those Louboutins?" His eyes widened.

"Yes! And they were half off and then an extra seventy-five percent off of that!"

"Wow. What an awesome deal. They look good on you." He smiled.

We started off with a glass of Chardonnay while we waited for our dinner. My mind was in overdrive with excitement and I couldn't wait for him to ask me. His apartment was much bigger than mine and had way more closet space. As I stared at him from across the table, I could tell he was nervous because his eye was twitching.

"So what did you want to discuss with me?" I asked with a grin.

He reached across the table and took hold of my hand.

"You know I love you, right?"

"Yes. Of course I do." My heart started to race.

"You're my best friend and we are so good together."

"I know we are." I smiled, waiting patiently for him to spit it out.

As his blue eyes intently stared into mine, he gave my hand a gentle squeeze.

"Chloe, friends are all we can ever be."

"What?" I cocked my head in confusion. "I don't understand, Corey."

He took in a long, deep breath. "What I'm trying to tell you is that I'm gay, Chloe."

I couldn't help the laughter that escaped me.

"Yeah, right. Come on, Corey. You wanted to talk about moving in together. You don't have to be so nervous about it. In fact, I'll make it easy for you. Yes, I would love to move in with you."

"Chloe, didn't you hear what I said. I'm serious. I'm gay. I'm sorry."

Tears filled my eyes as I silently shook inside. I pulled my hand away from his as I looked up at the ceiling to avoid the embarrassment of the tears that were about to fall in front of a restaurant filled with people.

"Chloe, talk to me. Please don't cry," he begged.

After a few moments of silence, an anger tore through me like a hurricane traveling over the ocean making its way to destroy whatever was in its path.

"How could you do this to me?" I asked through gritted teeth. "Why now? Why didn't you tell me this nine months ago? Why did you stay in a relationship with me if your sexuality was in question?" I spoke in a loud voice and the couple sitting at the table next to us glanced over.

"Will you keep your voice down?" he spoke calmly. "I didn't tell you this to hurt you. I'm being honest with you before things go any further."

"Any further?" I angrily spoke. "You had nine months to tell me. Why now, Corey?"

He looked down and slowly closed his eyes.

"Oh my God! You've met someone. Haven't you?" I barked at him across the table, and suddenly, all eyes in the restaurant were on us.

"Not here, Chloe."

His attempt to silence me to avoid causing him any further embarrassment pissed me off even more. I threw my napkin on the table and stood up.

"Not here? Really, Corey? How did you think I'd react to this news? Did you think if you told me in a public place that I would graciously accept it with a smile and walk away quietly? I gave you nine months of my life. I gave you my heart and you took it." The tears started rolling down my face. "You took my heart, knowing that you could never give me yours. I do believe that is the cruelest thing anyone has ever done to me. I guess the joke is on me. Have a nice life, Corey." I turned on my heels and stomped out of the restaurant.

I was shaking so bad that I couldn't walk down the street to my car, so I took a seat on a bench outside the restaurant. As I sat there with tears streaming down my face, trying to make sense of the last nine months of my life, Corey sat down beside me.

"I'm so sorry, Chloe. I never meant to hurt you."

"Go away, Corey." I wiped my eyes.

"I love you. You have to believe me. We are so good together as friends and I don't want to lose you."

Even though I was hurt and angry as hell, there was a sincerity in his voice that calmed me.

"What's his name?" I asked.

"Travis."

"I hate that name."

Corey chuckled.

"How long have you known?"

"Pretty much my whole life. I just kept trying to deny it and, every day, I became more miserable."

"Thanks." I shot him a look as I sniffled.

He hooked his arm around me and I laid my head on his shoulder.

"Don't take it like that, Chloe. You make me happy but not in a romantic relationship way. Does that make sense?"

I nodded my head. "I guess."

"You're a beautiful, smart, and fun woman, and you deserve someone who is not gay and who will love you like you deserve to be loved. I wanted to tell you now, not for my own sake, but for yours. With you leaving for London in a couple of weeks, I wanted you to be free in case you met someone."

"That was kind of you," I spoke in a sarcastic tone.

"Hey. I know it hurts, babe. It hurts me too. This is the last thing I wanted to tell you. But I had no choice. I couldn't live like this anymore."

"I get that. I really do." I lifted my head. "But I'm so hurt right now and I need a couple of days to process all of this."

"I understand." He looked at me as sadness filled his eyes.

I got up from the bench, and as I started to walk away, Corey reached out and grabbed my hand.

"I don't want to lose our friendship. You're too important to me, Chloe."

I pursed my lips together and slowly gave him a nod before heading home and collapsing into my bed.

Chapter 1

Two Weeks Later

"Cheer up, Chloe," Sienna, my best friend, pouted as we sat and sipped coffee in the airport.

"I am cheery. See?" I displayed a fake smile.

"Did you bring your list?" she asked as she held out her hand.

I sighed as I pulled it out of my purse and handed it to her. She took a pen from her purse and wrote something on it.

"What are you doing?" I asked.

"There." She turned the paper around.

Narrowing my eyes at her, I spoke, "Have sex with a stranger in a foreign country? Are you crazy?"

"No. I'm not crazy. This is a list of things we planned to do and see in London. Take a risk, Chloe. Do something spontaneous. Haven't you ever fantasized about having sex with a total stranger?"

"Umm. No!"

"Well, I have, and you should too."

"You do have sex with strangers. How is that fantasizing? Half the time, you don't even bother to get their name first."

"That may be and that's because names are never important. But I've never had sex with a stranger in a foreign country."

"That's because you've never been to another country."

"True. Just think about it for a minute. Sex with a man who is a mystery. No names, no getting to know each other first, not one bit of personal information. Just a couple of hours of pure pleasure and then you leave and never see him again. It's simple." She smirked.

Of course it was simple for Sienna. She was the queen of one-night stands. It was something she'd made a career out of. I've told her that she was a nymphomaniac. She laughed and said she wasn't and that she was just a woman who loved having sex with different men. With her five-foot-eight stature, hourglass-shaped figure, long black hair, and bright blue eyes, guys drooled whenever she walked past them.

"You make it sound like prostitution." I frowned.

Rolling her eyes, she spoke, "It's not prostitution, Chloe, and believe me, you could use some mind-blowing sex. I know for a fact you've never experienced it. Remember Johnathan?" Her brow arched. "The one who could only finish off with his hand whether you had an orgasm or not? Oh, and that guy named Kirk. Remember him? The freak who hated foreplay and just always crammed his dick inside you, missionary style, may I add, without making sure you were ready. Remember how sore you always were and walked like you had a stick up your ass for a few days? He was only out to satisfy himself. I know I don't need to mention sex with Corey. No matter how hard he tried, he just couldn't get into it with you. And you know why? Because he was gay and preferred ass over vagina."

I sat there, shaking my head at her in disgust.

"Oh and let's not forget Alfie. The guy who could never stay hard because every time you'd try to have sex, he thought of his mother and lost his boner." She laughed uncontrollably.

"Hey. Alfie was a nice guy. He just had some mommy issues that he needed to work out. And besides, we had sex once." I brought my coffee cup to my lips.

"One time, Chloe. One time in the six months you dated." She held up her index finger. "See; that's my point. You need to let go of the notion that you need to know a guy before you fuck him. It's much better if you don't know anything about him, like two strangers connecting for a brief moment in time who will never see each other again. It's all about the thrill. Keep calm and fuck a stranger." The smile on her face grew wide.

"I've said it before and I'll say it again, Sienna. You are a sex addict."

"I am not. I just like sex."

"I like sex too."

"You don't even know what real sex is, Chloe."

"YES I DO! How can you say that to me?"

"I'm entitled because I'm your best friend. And as your best friend, it's my job to make sure your lady parts are screaming with pleasure by a total stranger. So the next time you have sex, it will be with a mystery man in London."

15

I rolled my eyes as they called our flight for boarding. This was our last layover and now we were heading straight to London. Sitting on the plane, Sienna looked over at the cute guy that was sitting across the aisle from her and elbowed me. I looked at her as she tilted her head towards him.

"What?"

"He's hot and he's going to London. Maybe you can hook up with him."

"Stop it! I'm not hooking up with anyone."

"He keeps looking over at you. He's trying to be sly about it, but he's miserably failing."

"He's looking at you, not me."

Suddenly, she did the unthinkable.

"Excuse me. Could you please settle a debate between me and my best friend?"

"Sure," the guy replied.

"Are you staring at her or at me?"

I took in a deep breath and tried to hold it as long as I could with the hopes of passing out to avoid this embarrassing situation.

"I think you're both beautiful women." He smiled.

"Why, thank you. I'm Sienna, and this is Chloe." She extended her hand.

"Nice to meet you, Sienna." He reached over and extended his arm across Sienna. "Nice to meet you, Chloe." He flashed a big smile and spoke in his English accent, "I'm Sam."

I gulped over his accent. I wasn't expecting that.

"You're from England?" Sienna flirted and gave her "I want to fuck you" smile.

"Yes, and you're from?"

"We're both from New York, but Chloe lives in Los Angeles now."

"Ah. I see. So the two of you met up for a fancy vacation in England?"

"Yes. It's a place we've always wanted to visit and for good reason," she spoke.

The two of them carried on a conversation before and after we took off. About an hour into the flight, Sienna slipped her eye mask over her eyes and went to sleep. She claimed she was tired, but it was no doubt due to the four whiskey sours she drank; two before we took off and two right after we took off. We had been planning this trip for over a year. Being an assistant art curator, I didn't make very much money and living in Los Angeles was expensive, but I made sacrifices and saved almost every penny I made, including the money my parents sent to me for my birthday. The highlight of this trip for Sienna was bedding an Englishman, which I was sure she was already planning with Sam. The highlight for me was visiting the art galleries and museums to see the paintings that I'd only read about in books. I could care less about the men there or any man, period. After this last break-up, it became clearer than ever that I had bad luck when it came to men, so I made a vow to concentrate on my career, advancing to an art curator and enjoying life on my terms and my terms only. Fuck men and relationships. The minute I stepped off this plane and my feet hit the concrete of London, England, I was going to become a new woman. Possibly a woman who was going to have sex with a stranger in a foreign country.

Chapter 2

Six nights and seven days in London were coming to an end and it made me sad. We spent hours in the museums and galleries, shopped, took in all the beautiful sights London had to offer, and ate at some pretty amazing restaurants.

"Since tonight is our last night here, and I have unsuccessfully gotten you laid, we're going to dress in our finest and head down to the hotel bar for a while," Sienna spoke as she threw herself back on her bed.

I rolled my eyes. "What time is Sam meeting you down there?"

"What?" she asked as she propped herself up on her elbows. "How did you know?"

"I overheard your phone conversation in the bathroom this morning."

"Oh. I thought you were sleeping."

"I was until I heard you referring to his dick as an exploding cannon."

"Well, tonight's the night I will cross off on my list 'sex with a stranger in a foreign country.'"

"And why did it take you so long? We've been here a week. Where has he been all this time?"

"He's been busy with work and he lives an hour outside London. But tonight he's free and he's getting himself a room."

"You mean he's getting the two of you a room." I glared at her.

"Whatever. We'll still be in the hotel, so if you need me, just call."

"So what am I supposed to do tonight?"

"You're hanging out in the bar with us. Then, when we go back to his room, you can either stay down and tell the bartender what a man hater you are, pick up some hot guy, or come back up to the room and watch a movie."

"I like the man hater idea." I smiled.

She rolled her eyes and threw a pillow at me.

I slipped into my off-the-shoulder, cream-colored, short chiffon lace dress, then stepped into my matching heels and stood outside the bathroom door.

"Well, how do I look?" I asked Sienna, who was in the middle of applying her fake eyelashes.

"Adorable. Did you make sure to shave down there in case you meet a man tonight?"

I sighed. "Yes, Mother."

"Good girl." She looked down at her phone. "Shit, Sam is already waiting at the bar. He said he got us a table."

"Then you better hurry up. You don't want to keep your prince waiting. Oh, and by the way, Sam isn't a stranger, so you can't cross that off your list. You already broke your rule about knowing his name."

"He's a semi-stranger. I only know that he's twenty-eight and his name is Sam. I don't know anything else about him, so in a way, that counts."

I sighed as I sprayed some of my Victoria Secret perfume across my body.

About fifteen minutes after Sienna received Sam's text message, we headed down to the bar. As soon as we stepped inside the door, Sam stood up and waved us over to the table where he was sitting.

"Damn, he looks incredibly delicious," Sienna spoke with a grin. "I can't wait to taste him."

"Ugh." I shook my head.

After receiving a kiss on both cheeks, I took a seat across from Sam while Sienna practically sat in his lap. While I was sipping on my wine and watching the people come and go, I nearly choked to death when I spotted a man walk in and take a seat at the bar. Not just any ordinary man, but a man who was devastatingly handsome and the sexiest looking man my green eyes ever laid eyes on. He was tall, a little over six feet. His brown hair, which was styled with a matte spiked look, accented his almond-shaped eyes (too far away to see the exact color, but I was almost positive they were chocolate brown). The standard stubble he sported on his masculine jawline was pure perfection, as were his high cheekbones and perfectly straight nose. His skin was tanned and his tailored clothes left his body to the unimaginable. I bit down on my bottom lip as I stared at his back from the table. Sienna caught me and immediately took my attention.

"What are you staring at?"

"Nothing." I looked at her as I sipped my wine. "I was just watching the people come and go."

Her right eye narrowed at me and she could tell I was lying. She looked around the area but didn't seem to notice him.

"Well, we're going to go up to Sam's room now. Are you heading back to our room?"

"No. I think I'll stay down here for a while and have another glass of wine. I don't want to go up just yet."

Her eye narrowed at me again.

"You're more than welcome to come up to my room with us." Sam smiled. "Believe me, I wouldn't object."

Douchebag.

"Thanks for the offer, Sam, but I'm fine right where I am."

"Okay, sweetie. Enjoy the rest of your night and don't leave the hotel."

"Yes, Mother." I smiled.

She hooked her arm in Sam's and the two of them left. My eyes diverted back to the mystery man sitting at the bar. My mind pondered the thought of whether or not I should go and sit next to him. As I finished the last sip of wine and started to be brave to do the unthinkable, he got up from the bar stool and left. *Fuck.*

With a pout, I grabbed my wine glass and purse and sat down in the seat that was next to his.

"Refill, please." I pushed the glass towards the bartender.

"What's wrong? Your friends ditch you?" he asked in his sexy accent.

I sighed. "Pretty much. You know what? Forget the wine. Give me an orgasm."

The bartender smiled at me. "One orgasm coming right up, pretty lady." He winked.

"Did I just hear him right?" the devastatingly handsome man asked with his American accent as he sat down next to me.

My heart picked up its beat and my body started to sweat. He was even sexier up close. And his eyes; I was right. They were a dreamy chocolate brown that made me melt.

"Yes, you heard right," I nervously replied.

"Ah. You're American."

"Full blooded and all." I smiled like an idiot.

Why the hell did I just say that?

He ordered a bourbon and pulled out his phone. Glancing over at his left hand, I saw that there was no sign that a ring had ever been worn on that well-manicured finger of his.

"One orgasm for the beautiful American girl." The bartender grinned as he set down my drink in front of me.

"Her orgasm is on me," the man sitting next to me spoke. "Put it on my tab."

23

"Oh no. You don't have to buy my drink," I spoke in embarrassment.

"If there's one thing I'm excellent at giving, it's an orgasm. So enjoy." He smiled and my panties soaked themselves.

Shit. Why would he say that? He was definitely flirting. This could be my chance. I gulped. Sex with him would be intense. I could tell. The way he carried himself with such confidence told me he excelled at anything he did.

"I bet you do." I grinned as I held up my glass.

His eyes raked over me as the corners of his mouth curved into a cunning smile.

"Are you here with anyone?" he asked. "Perhaps a boyfriend?"

"Nope." I took a sip of my drink.

"That's a beautiful dress you're wearing."

"Thank you."

"What's your name?"

Don't tell him, Chloe. No names. No personal information. Nothing. It's all about the thrill. The mystery man. Keep him a stranger.

"My name isn't important and neither is yours," I spoke in a seductive voice.

He cocked his head to the side with a beautiful grin across his face as he stared into my eyes. Placing his hand on my thigh, which caused my body to spasm, he spoke, "Are you staying at this hotel?"

"Yes." I looked down at his hand.

"Me too." He leaned close to my ear as his hot breath swept across my skin. "How about we take our drinks up to my room? Perhaps you'd like an orgasm or two in private." His hand made its way up my dress and stopped when he reached the fabric of my panties. I gasped as it felt like my heart went into cardiac arrest.

"Sounds fun." I smiled. I couldn't believe I just used the word "fun."

Chapter 3

He placed his hand on the small of my back as we entered the elevator and took it to the top floor. Nerves flooded every fiber of my body and I couldn't believe I was actually going to go through with this. I needed to maintain composure and behave like a woman who had done this sort of thing before. But I hadn't and that was the problem. What if I totally sucked and disappointed him? Did it really matter, though? I was doing this for me, not him, and I'd never see him again anyway, so who cared, right? *Right*, I silently thought to myself.

Upon entering his suite, I was enthralled at how beautiful it was. My room was just standard and blah.

"I had no idea they had rooms like this here," I spoke as I set my purse down on the black leather couch.

"It's their finest suite." He smiled as he took the glass from my hand and set it down.

I walked over to the window and looked out over the city of London. Suddenly, I felt his hand push my hair to the side and the trail of his sweltering breath grazed my neck.

"You are a very beautiful woman." His lips delicately pressed against my skin, making my body quiver in ecstasy.

"Thank you." I smiled as I tilted my head, giving him easier access.

His hands roamed up and down the sides of my body before turning me around to face him.

"I want your name." His lips brushed gently against mine.

"No names and no personal information about each other. Tonight is my last night here."

He arched his brow as a small smile crossed his perfectly shaped lips.

"Mine too."

"So names aren't important."

"I suppose you're right." His mouth smashed into mine.

The way he kissed me was not natural. Or maybe it was and I'd just been kissed the wrong way all these years. His tongue parted my lips and entered my mouth, leaving me breathless, dazed, and confused. I had forgotten I was a girl from L.A. who had just been dumped by her gay boyfriend. Tonight, I was a sexy woman, having a one-night stand with an incredibly gorgeous man in another country. A man who made me feel something I had never felt before.

"Take off your dress and let me see that gorgeous body of yours," he spoke in a low voice as he broke our kiss.

He took a step back and watched as I kicked off my shoes and stripped out of my dress. A growl escaped him as I stood there in my cream-colored lace panties and matching strapless bra. He walked over to me with a hunger in his eyes. Placing his hands firmly on my hips, he turned me around so I was facing the window.

"Don't worry. Nobody can see anything up here," he spoke as he unhooked my bra and slid his tongue along my spine while his hands firmly grasped my breasts.

My body trembled beneath his fingers as my heart pounded in my chest. A pool of warmth engulfed me down below and the throbbing became fierce. After exploring my ass cheeks with his mouth, he turned me around so I was facing him. He was on his knees and his eyes met the top of my panties.

"Fuck, you are so sexy," he moaned while his fingers gently took them down. His tongue licked up my inner thigh while his fingers drifted across my opening. "You are so wet and so beautiful," he whispered as his tongue slid up and down my most sensitive spot.

I no longer cared about anything in the world. I only cared about how good he made me feel and how I'd probably never recover after being fucked by him. My hands ran through his hair as he dipped his finger inside me while his tongue circled my clit. I could feel myself swelling against him. My breath hitched as an explosion of pleasure erupted and I felt like I was going to collapse. He stood up and, in one swoop, I was in his arms as he carried me over to the bed. Gently laying me down, his eyes never left mine as he stripped out of his clothes. His body. My eyes couldn't tear themselves away from his toned and muscular form. From his biceps to his chest, his washboard abs and his perfectly sculpted V-line sent my body into hyper drive. When he pulled down his underwear, I gulped at the sight of him. He was perfectly shaven and his cock stood tall, thick, and proud.

He walked towards the bed and climbed on top of me, taking my hardened nipple into his mouth, sucking and nipping before moving over to the other one. His fingers dipped inside me once again, moving easily in and out, causing the wetness to pour out of me. His tongue slid down my abdomen and stopped at my belly button as it made circles around it, causing spasms so severe I thought I was going to die. Words weren't spoken. We were both caught up in the heat of the moment, a heat that radiated from the both of us. His mouth made his way down to my pussy as he took hold of my legs and spread them wide. I threw my head back in appreciation at how this man made me feel.

"You taste so fucking good, and as much as I would love to sit here and devour you all night, I have to fuck you."

He stood up and reached inside his wallet, pulling out a condom. Tearing the corner with his mouth, he removed it from the wrapper and gracefully slid it over his throbbing cock. Nothing had ever turned me on as watching him do that did. He climbed on top of me and kissed me before thrusting himself inside me, inch by inch. We both let out a moan as he buried himself deep within me.

"God, you're tight. Ah. You feel so good." He thrusted in and out of me. "Do you like the way my cock feels inside you?"

"Yes," I wailed as his thrusting became rapid.

Our mouths met once again and our tongues tangled with passion as low moans escaped us.

He rolled over on his back, pulling me on top of him effortlessly.

"Sit up and fuck me," he commanded. "I want to see that beautiful body ride me."

I sat up like he asked, my hands firmly planted on his chest as he grabbed hold of my breasts, kneading them and fingering my nipples while my hips ground into him.

"So beautiful," he moaned.

Our eyes locked onto each other as I moved back and forth.

"That's it, baby. Fuck me nice and hard."

He grabbed the back of my head and pulled me down as he passionately kissed me. Breaking our kiss, I sat up and circled my hips as my body went into an orgasmic state and I let go, giving into another orgasm. He quickly flipped me over and took me from behind, pounding into me with long, deep strokes as his hands firmly grasped my ass. A hiss escaped him as he halted and then slowly moved inside of me as he came.

He collapsed on top of me and softly kissed my shoulder as we both tried to regain our breath. My world had just been rocked by this one man. A stranger whom I'd just met a little over an hour ago. A stranger that I'd never see again but who had done something to me that I couldn't explain.

He climbed off and threw the condom in the trash.

"You can get under the covers," he spoke as I lay there, unable to move.

"Yeah, but I can't move."

"I didn't hurt you, did I?" he asked as he ran his hand down my back.

"No. You didn't hurt me at all. I just feel paralyzed at the moment."

He chuckled as he took hold of my hand and helped me up and under the sheets. I turned on my side, facing the other way. I wasn't sure why I did. I just couldn't bring myself to face him after what we had just done. Maybe it was the fact that if I looked at him, I would cry with happiness at the experience he gave me. Or maybe if I looked at him, I would become emotionally attached. As I lay there, his arms wrapped around me.

"Good night, beautiful strange girl." He softly kissed my shoulder.

"Good night, handsome strange guy."

Tomorrow morning was going to be awkward and I needed to make sure I escaped before he woke up.

Chapter 4

Him

She refused to tell me her name. Normally, I wouldn't care. But something inside me needed to know who she was. She was stunningly beautiful and a name would complete her. It didn't matter anyway. In the morning, I'd be gone before she woke up and I'd never see her again. It was probably for the best anyway. I would hurt her and she would ultimately hate me. It's what I did. It's all I knew. This feeling inside me as I held her scared me. I didn't know this girl at all and yet, I felt compelled to. I got the feeling she had never done this before, not with a total stranger. She was nervous. That much I could tell. She still was nervous. I closed my eyes and I could still see her. The way her body trembled with the mere touch of my hand excited me. Her blonde hair with the curled ends that draped over her shoulders looked like silk and her green eyes that looked like jade stared into mine as I fucked her. Her body: slender, toned, yet fragile. She was the perfect height at five foot seven and even more perfect in those sexy stiletto heels she wore. Her scent infiltrated my senses. She smelled liked roses, a scent that would always remind me of this night.

The next morning, I quietly climbed out of bed and put on my clothes. If I showered, it would wake her and I needed to leave before she awoke. My suitcase was already packed and ready to go. As I grabbed my watch from the nightstand, I stared at her. She looked like an angel, sound asleep and exhausted from last night when we fucked again. I wanted to kiss her goodbye, but for fear of waking her, I didn't. I grabbed a piece of paper from the desk and jotted down a few words.

"Good bye, beautiful stranger," I whispered as I grabbed my suitcase and quietly walked out the door.

Chapter 5

Chloe

My eyes flew open and, for a second, I couldn't remember where I was. I looked over to the other side of the bed; it was empty. I sat up and looked around. There didn't appear to be any sign of him. Climbing out of bed, I slipped on the robe that was hanging on the back of the bedroom door and quietly walked into the living area of the suite. He wasn't anywhere. I noticed when I walked back into the bedroom that the suitcase I saw sitting in the corner last night was gone. He had left. Glancing over at the dresser, I saw a note. Picking it up, I sat down on the edge of the bed.

"Thank you for a beautiful night. Have a safe trip home."

I took in a deep breath and let it out. I picked my clothes up off the floor, grabbed my purse, and headed back to my room. Just as I inserted the card key, I heard Sienna coming down the hall.

"What are you doing?" she asked.

"Oh, nothing." I opened the door and stepped inside.

"Why are you wearing that robe and why are you carrying your—Holy shit on a cracker, you had sex last night!" she yelled.

"Shh." I held my finger to my lips.

"Don't you tell me to shush. You better tell me who, what, when, where, and why, right now!"

"I will. Can I make a cup of this pathetic shit they call coffee?"

"Hell no! Fuck the coffee. You are telling me exactly what happened right now!"

Sitting down on the bed, I cupped my face in my hands.

"Chloe, he didn't hurt you, did he?"

Shaking my head, I looked up at her.

"No. Just the opposite. I can't explain how he made me feel."

With a small smile, Sienna sat down on the bed and hooked her arm around me.

"It was that good, huh?"

"Mind-blowing. Superb. Breathtaking. Fantastic."

"Okay. Okay. I get it. Now tell me who this mind-blowing man was."

"The most incredible and perfect-looking man I've ever seen in my life," I spoke as I looked at her.

"Name?"

"I didn't get his name. No names, remember?" I cocked my head.

"Shit. I didn't teach you right. If he's that incredibly good-looking, it's always good to put a name with the body."

Rolling my eyes, I sighed. "We didn't exchange names. We just exchanged passion and, oh my God, Sienna, he was—I'd never felt—the orgasms were—"

"Wow. I have never seen you like this before. What the fuck did he do to you?"

I got up from the bed and walked into the bathroom to start the shower. She followed behind.

"He was gentle and sweet and he said things to me no other man ever had."

"You made sure he used a condom, right?"

"Yes. He used a condom."

"How many orgasms?" She smiled.

"I lost count." I bit down on my bottom lip.

"So how did you leave it with him this morning?" she asked, leaning up against the sink.

"I woke up and he was gone. I found this note on the dresser." I pulled the note from my robe pocket and handed it to her.

After reading it, she looked at me and clasped my shoulders.

"Congratulations, Chloe, on becoming a full-fledged woman."

"Get out of here," I lightly smacked her hand.

"Don't be too long. We have to pack and head to the airport."

Stepping into the shower, I realized I had forgotten to ask her about Sam.

"How was Sam last night?" I yelled.

"Nothing like I expected. A bit disappointing. He's rather sloppy in bed. I had to take control and I wasn't happy about it."

I laughed as I shampooed my hair. There was nothing sloppy about the man I was with last night. He was perfect and always in control.

****

Landing in Boston, Sienna and I hugged good bye. She had a flight to catch back to New York and I had a flight back to L.A.

"I hate leaving you." She pouted.

"I know." My eyes began to tear. "I wish I could move back to New York."

"Then do it! Besides me, your parents would be thrilled."

"There aren't any jobs available. I've been looking."

"Then maybe you need to switch careers."

"You know I can't and won't. I love art too much."

She looked at her watch and gave me another hug. "I'm boarding in five minutes. I'll skype you later tonight."

"Bye, Sienna. Have a safe flight."

"Bye, sweets. You too."

Dragging my carry-on behind me, I headed to my gate. My flight didn't board for another hour, so I stopped and grabbed a coffee. I moved to Los Angeles a year ago when I landed a job at an art gallery as an assistant art curator. I had just graduated with my master's degree, and the owner of the art gallery that I interned for in New York offered me the job at his L.A. gallery. I really didn't have a choice. There was no position for me in New York and I needed a job. Leaving Sienna and my parents behind was the hardest thing I had ever done, but being on my own in L.A. was a great experience. I had always been independent and I adapted quickly and made a few new friends. But Sienna and I would be best friends for life. She was like my sister. We shared everything and we skyped every single night or facetimed. That was what calls were: facetime. We very rarely did regular phone calls.

Stepping off the plane at LAX, I headed to baggage claim and saw Corey standing there holding up a sign with my name on it.

"You dork." I smiled as I hugged him.

"How was London?"

"Fabulous. We had the best time, and the galleries and museums over there are to die for. You would have loved it."

"I'm sure I would have," he spoke as he grabbed my suitcase from the belt. "So did you meet any hot Englishmen over there?"

I shrugged. "A couple but—" I smiled.

Corey looked over at me with a small grin. "But?"

"I met an American man. A really hot and sexy American man."

"Oh. His name, please."

"I didn't get his name. We just had wild and amazing sex and the next morning, he was gone."

I continued walking and then stopped when I noticed Corey was no longer next to me.

Turning around, I spoke, "What? Why did you stop?"

"You, Chloe Kane, had sex with a man and didn't get his name first? What's the matter with you? Who are you?" He smiled.

"It was on my list."

"What was on your list?" he asked as we continued walking.

"Sex with a stranger in a foreign country."

He slowly shook his head. "You're weird. He could have been dangerous, Chloe."

"Oh, he was deliciously dangerous." I grinned.

****

It felt good to be back home. After I showered, I made a cup of tea and curled up on the couch, still thinking about the man from last night. No matter how hard I tried, I couldn't get him out of my head or the feel of him on my body. Every time I touched my lips, I could still feel them trembling from his kiss.

As I was fantasizing about him, my phone rang with a facetime call from Sienna.

"Hello, lovely." I smiled.

"Look at you, all cozy in your jammies already."

"As much fun as I had in London, I'm happy to be home."

"Me too. Sam keeps texting me. He said he misses me already and wants to plan a trip to New York to come and visit." She rolled her eyes.

"Are you going to let him?" I asked as I sipped my tea.

"I don't know. Even though sex with him was utterly boring, I kind of like his company. How are you doing? After that wild night of sex, you must still be thinking about that hot man."

"No, I'm not. He's a distant memory now."

"You're lying. I know you, Chloe, and you get involved, even though I clearly try to teach you differently."

I sighed. "Okay. So what? I am still thinking about him and I can't help it. I just wish I would have gotten his name."

"Tsk tsk." She waved her finger. "Goes against the stranger rule. Besides, even if you did get his name, what were you going to do? Stalk him? Google him? Find a thousand guys with the same name in the US and then call them one by one, asking if they were the sexy guy who made you orgasm multiple times in London?"

"Why do you have to be like that?" I rolled my eyes.

"You love me and you know it. Anyway, I just wanted to check in and make sure you made it home safe. I have to go shower because I need to be at work bright and early tomorrow morning. I have a big client coming in and his demands for the perfect ad are annoying, so I have to be on top of my game."

"Have a good night and we'll talk tomorrow. Good luck with your meeting."

"Thanks, love. Ta ta."

Chapter 6

Two Months Later

Arriving at work, I set my bag down as Silas called over to me.

"Chloe, Mr. Black is here and wants to talk to you."

"Really? I didn't know he was coming."

"We didn't either. He was here before us."

Walking into the back office, I smiled when I saw him sitting behind the desk.

"Good morning, Connor. Welcome back to L.A. Silas said you wanted to see me."

"Good morning, Chloe. Have a seat." He smiled.

Taking a seat across from his desk, I was a little nervous as to why he was here and why he wanted to talk to me. I didn't think I was in trouble for anything because my work was impeccable. Oh God, maybe he was laying me off. A thousand reasons were swimming around in my mind and it started to worry me.

"You've been working here for a little over a year now, correct?" he asked.

"Yes."

"Do you like it here, Chloe?"

I thought that was a strange question to ask and he caught me off guard.

"Yes. Very much."

"More than New York?"

"Well, my friends and family are in New York and I miss them, but so far, L.A. is working for me." I smiled.

"Have you made friends here?"

"Some."

"Are you currently seeing anyone?"

Okay, now this was getting weird as far as I was concerned.

"No," I replied in confusion.

He chuckled. "Okay, I'll get right to the point. I can see you're getting a little irritated with all my questions. How would you like to move back to New York?"

I was stunned by his question. "Are you serious?" I asked with a hint of excitement.

"Yes. I'm opening up a new art gallery. Much bigger than the one you interned at and way bigger than this one. The reason I offered you this position here is because I didn't want to let you go, but at the time, I didn't have anything available in New York. You're an excellent employee, Chloe, and Ellery and I would love for you to manage the new gallery. Your passion for art and history is exactly what this new gallery needs. You did such a great job when you interned for us and, to be honest, Ellery was quite pissed at me for not creating a position for you in New York. I thought it would be best for you to work here for a while. You passed the test. You've done an outstanding job helping out, but you aren't developing your full potential being an assistant."

I sat there in shock as I listened to his praise. Words wouldn't escape my lips. I felt like I was dreaming and any moment I'd wake up in my bed.

"Aren't you going to say anything?" He smiled.

"I would be honored to run your gallery back in New York. I'm sorry, Connor, but this is such a shock to me. I wasn't expecting this."

"A good shock, I hope."

"Of course. New York is my home and I'd love to move back there."

"Good. I was hoping you'd say that. Ellery will be extremely pleased. How soon can you move back?"

"I don't know. I still have my lease here for another three months on my apartment."

He waved his hand in front of his face. "Don't worry about your lease. I'll take care of it. I would like you back in New York as soon as possible. Even as early as next week. I will hire a moving company to move your belongings, so you don't have to worry about that. You'll be on a salary with health benefits, vacation time, sick time, and a 401k plan."

"Wow. I don't know what to say. Thank you, Connor. Something like this has always been my dream."

"You're welcome, Chloe. I have the gallery scheduled to open in a couple of months. That should give you plenty of time to get settled and get everything set up. I want the opening of this gallery to be the biggest and best, so the work involved is going to be quite intense."

"I know, and I promise you that I can handle it."

"I know you can." He smiled. "That's why I offered you the job. Also, I'm going to have my realtor get in touch with you. He's one of the best and he can help you find an apartment. In fact, I'll text him your phone number now." He pulled his phone from his pocket and grinned. "I received a text message from Ellery asking if you took the job."

"You can tell her that I fully accept and I can't wait to get back to New York."

"I certainly will."

"Connor, I have one question."

"What is it?" he asked as he turned around before walking out the door.

"Why are you opening up another gallery in New York?"

"For Ellery, of course." He winked.

As soon as he left, I did a happy dance and silently screamed as I jumped up and down. I couldn't believe that I was moving back to New York. My parents and Sienna were going to be so happy.

****

Saying goodbye to Corey was hard, but he promised to come to New York and visit. This was a new start for me. It felt like the beginning of a new life. My parents were beyond thrilled that I was moving back and staying with them until I found an apartment. They told me just to live with them and they promised to give me my privacy. As much as I loved my parents more than anything in the world, living with them permanently wasn't an option. They were, how do I say it, a little different from your average parents. They were modern hippies. Throwbacks from the sixties living in today's modern world. Being the free-spirits they were, growing up was a lot of fun, but also embarrassing at times. When I called and told them about Corey, they were happy for him, that he finally re-birthed himself and accepted who he really was. I agreed, but the way they said it was as if I shouldn't have been hurt or upset by it. I spent nine months with him in a relationship. As happy as I was now for him, it did hurt a lot when he told me.

As soon as the plane landed at JFK, I stepped off and took in the New York City air. It was good to be back home.

"There's our baby girl," my mom shouted as she ran to me. My dad followed behind.

"Hi, Mom. Dad." I hugged them both.

"Do you have any idea how happy we are to have you home?" She hugged me tightly again.

"Yeah. Actually, I do." I tried to breathe.

My dad grabbed my two suitcases and we hailed a taxi back to their apartment. Stepping into my childhood bedroom, I smiled. I'd forgotten how much I'd missed this room when I was in L.A. As I started to unpack, I heard a knock on the door and a voice that was music to my ears. Running out of my room, I ran to Sienna and threw my arms around her.

"Thank God you're home for good. I'm sorry I couldn't be at the airport. That damn meeting I was in ran late."

"Don't worry about it." I smiled.

"Hi, Sienna," my mom spoke. "You're just in time for dinner. I've made a vegetarian macaroni and cheese."

Sienna made a face at me. She wasn't fond of my mother's cooking, but being the sometimes polite woman she was, she graciously smiled and took a seat at the table.

"So tell us how work is going, Sienna," my mom asked as she scooped some macaroni and cheese onto her plate.

"Oh, the usual. My coworkers are backstabbing bitches, my boss won't stop hitting on me, and one of my clients hated the advertising campaign that took me two months to develop. But overall, it's going well." She smiled.

"Are you seeing anyone?" my father asked.

"No. Not really. I did meet this guy on the plane on our way to London. He lives there. He's supposed to come to New York to visit next month."

"He is?" I looked at her in shock. "You didn't tell me that."

"Oh. Guess what? Sam is coming to visit next month. Too bad you don't know where Mr. Sexy lives. You could have invited him and we could have double dated."

"Who's Mr. Sexy?" my mom asked.

"The guy she met in London. Didn't she tell you?" Sienna opened her big mouth.

"No," my dad replied. "Tell us about Mr. Sexy, Chloe."

I shot Sienna a look and she gave me the "oops" face. "I'm sorry. I thought you told them. You tell them everything."

She was right. I did tell my parents everything. We always had an open relationship and no subject was ever off limits. Hell, my mom was so sexually open that for my sixteenth birthday she bought me a vibrator. But I didn't mention what happened in London to them.

"He's just a guy I met at the hotel bar on our last night there. That's all."

"What's his name?" my mom asked.

"I didn't get his name."

"Why wouldn't you get his name?" my dad asked.

"Don't people who meet usually introduce themselves?" my mom chimed in.

"We had sex. I didn't want to know his name, and I didn't want to know anything about him. It was on my list." I took a bite of macaroni and cheese.

"What was on your list?" My mom cocked her head.

"To have sex with a stranger in a foreign country. We did. He was beyond amazing, and when I woke up the next morning, he was gone. So now you know. Can we please talk about something else?"

There it was. The reason I didn't tell my parents about him. The truth was not a day went by since that night that I hadn't thought about him. No matter how hard I tried to push him out of my mind, I couldn't. Even though I planned on leaving him before he woke up, it bothered me that he left first. Having sex with him affected me more emotionally than I thought it ever would have.

After dinner, I hugged Sienna goodbye and went to my room. My mom followed me and sat down on the edge of my bed while I hung up some clothes in my closet.

"Are you okay, Chloe? I can sense something is going on with you. Your chakras are all out of whack."

I sighed. "I'm fine, Mom. It's just ever since that night, that total stranger is all I seem to think about. Why can't I forget about him?" I sat down next to her, clutching a sweater in my hand. "It's been two months."

"Well, you said you had amazing sex, right?"

"Yeah." I smiled. "Totally like nothing I'd ever experienced with a man before."

"It sounds to me like the two of you had a connection. More than just physical." She kissed the side of my head. "Try not to think about him anymore and don't let your experience deter you from finding the right man. There are others out there. What's to be fated, will be. You know that. I'm teaching yoga tomorrow morning at eight o'clock. Why don't you come and clear your mind?"

"I can't. I'm meeting the realtor tomorrow morning and then I have to get to the gallery."

"Okay, sweetheart. Don't deviate from your spiritual well-being. You know how important it is."

I gave her a small smile as she walked out of the room.

Chapter 7

"Well, what do you think?" Jason, my realtor, asked as we walked around the apartment. "The best part is that it's within walking distance to the art gallery you'll be working at."

"I like it. I like that it's a brownstone, the apartment is on the second floor, and that it was built in the 1900s. The architecture is so beautiful. Oh, and I like that it's in my price range."

"Excellent. Would you like to fill out the renter's application?" He smiled.

"Yes. When would the apartment be ready to move into?"

"Next week. The owners are anxious because they're leaving for Italy for six months, so they want this taken care of before they leave."

"A week is perfect." I smiled.

The apartment was definitely a lot smaller than my place back in L.A., but this was New York and the spaces were small. When I stepped inside, I instantly felt at home. It was the kind of place where I could envision myself relaxing after a long day at the gallery.

Jason handed me the rental application and I filled it out on the spot and handed it to him.

"Perfect." He grinned. "I'll get this processed right away and let you know tomorrow. It was a pleasure to meet you, Miss Kane."

"Thank you, Jason. The pleasure was all mine."

As I stepped out onto West 82nd Street, I looked down at the tree-lined street. Pulling my phone from my purse, I facetimed Sienna. Her stressed face appeared on the screen.

"What's wrong?" I laughed.

"This client is driving me bat shit crazy. He'll be lucky if I don't go to his house and murder him in his sleep. Where are you?"

"This is West 82nd Street, where I found an apartment. Look at the brownstone." I held the phone up.

"Hey, I know that place. A girl that I work with used to live there. So when are you moving in?"

"The realtor is processing the application today and he'll let me know tomorrow. If everything is approved, I can move in next week."

"Woohoo. I'll help you and we can have a decorating party." She smiled.

"Sounds good. Listen, I'm going to head to the gallery now. I'll talk to you later."

"Bye, lover." She kissed the screen.

Laughing, I blew her a kiss and ended the call. When I reached the gallery, I stepped inside and smiled when I saw Ellery. The place was crawling with construction workers. Noise infiltrated the place as hammers banged against the walls and saws were going off every second.

"You're here!" she exclaimed as she walked over and hugged me. "Welcome home, Chloe."

"Thanks, Ellery. It's good to see you and it's great to be back in New York." I took hold of both her hands. "I can't thank you and Connor enough for giving me this opportunity."

"Don't mention it. You are an excellent worker with an incredible eye for art. You remind me of me when I was your age." She winked. "Come on, I'll show you around."

After walking around half of the 5,000-square-foot space, Ellery took me up the wrought-iron stairs that led to the second level.

"Up here is where your office is, the bathroom, and a kitchen area. What do you think?"

"I love it. It's perfect up here."

"Come and see your office." She took my hand and led me to a space that consisted of glass walls and a large glass door.

"Wow. This is beautiful," I spoke as I sat down behind the large L-shaped glass desk with the Apple computer sitting proudly on top.

"You should have everything you need. The file cabinets are being delivered tomorrow, so you can place those wherever you see fit. Also, I've ordered some couches, tables, and chairs to go in the space out there. You're going to love them. I went way over Connor's budget, but he doesn't need to know that." She smiled.

"I promise I won't tell him."

****

Settling into my new apartment was a piece of cake compared to the hustle and bustle of trying to get the art gallery ready for its grand opening reception tomorrow night. Everything was in place and ready to be seen. My main focus the last month was getting the gallery ready, leaving very little time for anything else, including a personal life. The good thing that came out of immersing myself in my work was the fact that I hadn't given one thought about the man from London. He had now become a distant memory in my mind. An incredible one-night stand that I had let affect me for too long was now buried and locked away.

After changing out of my work clothes and into something more casual, I grabbed my purse and headed to Bellini's, where I was meeting Sienna for dinner. As the cab pulled up to drop me off, I reached into my purse to pay the cab fare. Just as I was about to open the door and climb out, I froze.

"Ma'am, is everything okay?" the cab driver asked.

I gulped as my eyes stared at the handsome stranger from London. My heart began to race and the butterflies that had lain dormant awoke, causing a stir in my belly.

"Just give me a second," I spoke as I pulled up the hood to my jacket and took my sunglasses out of my purse, putting them on to hide myself from him.

Opening the door, I climbed out and kept my head down, but as I passed the two gentlemen standing and talking on the sidewalk, I slightly lifted my head so I could get a glimpse of his sultry chocolate eyes. Both men looked at me, probably wondering why the hell I was wearing sunglasses when it was almost dark out. He was just as gorgeous as I remembered him to be. As I made my way into the restaurant, Sienna was standing there waiting for me.

"Hey." I tapped her shoulder. "It's me."

She turned around and looked me up and down with an odd look on her face.

"What the hell are you doing? Why are you wearing that hat and sunglasses?"

Looking behind me and out the door, I saw he was gone.

"I saw him!" I whispered.

"Saw who?"

"Him! The stranger from London." I removed my sunglasses and hat.

"What? Where?" She looked over my shoulder.

"He was standing outside the restaurant talking to some guy. I had to hide myself so he didn't recognize me."

She placed her hand on my shoulder. "Are you sure it was him?"

"Positive. Do you think I'd ever forget him?"

The hostess walked up and told us our table was ready. After being seated, I told the hostess to tell our waitress that I needed a double shot of tequila ASAP.

"Why are you so nervous?" Sienna asked. "It's a miracle that he's here in New York and you saw him again. I have no clue why you hid yourself from him. You should have walked up and said, 'Hey, remember me? The girl from London who you had a night of wild sex with and then escaped the next morning without as so much as a goodbye?'"

Sinking back into the booth, I sighed. "Don't you get it? I can never see him again after that night."

"Why? It's not like you're entering a relationship with him. It was one night, Chloe. One satisfying night. If the two of you do run into each other, all you have to do is say hi and move along. And I don't mean to be rude, but he may not even remember you. He's a guy and he had random sex with a random girl. If he did it with you, I can guarantee he makes a habit of it. Do you think I remember half of the guys I fuck?" She smiled.

"Maybe you're right. He probably wouldn't remember me anyway."

"Finally, you get it. Now stop this neurotic behavior and let's enjoy dinner."

Chapter 8

I walked around the gallery, making sure everything was in order. The caterers had arrived and the bar was being set up. Nerves filtered through me, as this was one of the biggest nights of my life and I had to pull it off to perfection. Failure wasn't an option. As I took in a deep breath, Connor and Ellery walked over to me.

"You seem to be nervous." Connor smiled.

"I am. This is a big night and I'm worried."

"Do you think you did a good job?" Ellery asked.

"I think so."

"Then you have nothing to be nervous or worried about." Connor winked.

"Relax, Chloe. This is going to be a fabulous night and a huge success. Have a drink." Ellery pulled a glass of champagne off the tray as one of the waiters walked by.

One by one, the people started to enter the gallery. I watched the expressions on their faces as they moved from one area to another, looking at the vast collection of art. As I was talking to one of the artists, Sienna walked up and stood next to me.

"I am so proud of you." She smiled. "This place looks phenomenal."

"Thanks. It was a lot of work but well worth it."

"Are your mom and dad coming?" she asked as she grabbed an hors d'oeuvre from the tray.

"Yes. They should be here shortly."

As I brought my glass of champagne to my lips and took a small sip, it sprayed out of my mouth as my eyes looked over and saw him standing there with a beautiful tall brunette, looking at the Impressionist art collection.

"Chloe, are you all right?" Sienna asked with concern.

"NO. It's him."

"Where?" Her head turned in every direction.

"Right over there." I pointed.

"Holy shit. The hot guy with the brunette?"

"Yes."

My belly fluttered at the sight of him but turned sick when I looked at her.

"What the fuck is he doing here?" I asked as I ducked behind a large sculpture.

"He obviously likes art. Go talk to him. Maybe you can tell the fake brunette about your little rendezvous in London."

"NO! I need to go to my office for something. I'll be right back."

"Chloe. You aren't being cool right now."

I ran up the stairs to the second floor and tried to collect myself. This had to be the worst time for me to see him. Once I calmed down and took in a few deep breaths, I came to the realization that there was no way he'd remember me and I was acting like an anxiety-ridden child. Perhaps he didn't have a girlfriend when we hooked up. I mean, it had been four months and a man like that wouldn't be single for long. Or maybe that was his wife and he was in London on business and cheated on her with me. Maybe it was something he did when he was away from home. Now, in my mind, he was a total douchebag. I was acting ridiculous and if by some chance we did run into each other, I would pretend I didn't remember him. Taking in a deep breath, I slowly walked down the stairs with my head held high. This was my night and I wasn't going to let the likes of the stranger from London ruin it for me.

I saw Sienna and my parents standing over by the portable bar. Walking over, I hugged my mom and dad and thanked them for coming.

"Are you okay now?" Sienna asked.

"Yes. I am perfectly fine." I smiled.

"Good girl." She winked. "Now if you'll excuse us, your mom and dad have some art they would like to see."

"We'll talk to you later, sweetie, when you aren't so busy." My mom smiled as she touched my cheek.

I carefully scanned the gallery and didn't see him. Maybe he got bored and left. One could only hope.

"Do you have any Chardonnay?" I asked the cute bartender.

"I sure do. Would you like a glass?"

"If I didn't, I wouldn't have asked." I smiled.

As he poured the wine into a glass and handed it to me, Connor walked up from behind.

"Chloe, I would like you to meet someone."

Turning around, I gulped and my eyes widened as they locked with the sultry brown eyes of the man from London.

"Chloe, this is Sebastian Bennett. Sebastian, this is Chloe Kane, the talented woman responsible for putting this all together for me."

The corners of his mouth curved upwards as he held out his hand.

"It's nice to meet you, Chloe Kane."

Carefully extending my hand to his, the moment our skin touched, I felt a jolt of electricity course throughout my body. A jolt so electrifying that it left me breathless.

"It's nice to meet you as well, Mr. Bennett." I was barely able to get the words out.

"Please, call me Sebastian. You did a wonderful job. I was giving all the credit to Connor and he told me that you were the one who put this all together. I'm highly impressed." He smiled.

"Thank you."

Suddenly, the brunette appeared by his side.

"Sebastian, you must come and see this painting over here. It would look perfect in your home."

My heart was racing a mile a minute, for I knew he remembered me. I could tell by the expression on his face.

"Like I said, it was nice to meet you, Chloe," he spoke with a sly smile. He placed his hand on the brunette's back and they turned and walked away.

The air slowly started to return to my lungs as I made my way to the bathroom. Sebastian Bennett. After all these months of wondering his name, I now knew, and what a sexy name it was. When the brunette walked up to him, I quickly scanned her finger and saw there was no ring. As I was in the bathroom, I pulled out my phone and sent a text message to Sienna.

"You need to come to the bathroom now! He remembered me and his name is Sebastian Bennett."

"WTF! You met him? I'm on my way."

A few moments later, the bathroom door opened and Sienna walked in.

"What the hell happened and where was I?"

"Right after you left to go look at some art, Connor walked up with him and introduced us."

"Are you sure he remembered you?"

"Yes, he remembered me! It was obvious by the look on his face."

"So what did he say?"

"That it was nice to meet me and he was impressed."

"Impressed by what? Was he talking about that night?"

"NO! He was impressed about the gallery."

"Oh. Did you let on that you remembered him?"

"No, but I'm sure the expression on my face did."

She shrugged. "Relax. If he seeks you out again, pretend you don't know him and that night in London never happened. After tonight, you'll probably never see him again."

"Really? How can you stand there and say that? You're the one who said that he probably wouldn't remember me in the first place."

"Okay. So I was wrong. Now it's your turn. Pretend you don't remember a thing. Act like he's a stranger."

"He is a stranger!" I squealed.

"Not anymore. Now you know his name."

Rolling my eyes, I went back out to the crowded area and mingled with the patrons. Finally, the last guest left and I was exhausted. The opening was a huge success and I couldn't have been more pleased.

"You look exhausted," Ellery spoke as she walked over to me.

"I am. It was an amazing night."

"It sure was." Connor smiled. "You did an outstanding job. You should be very proud of yourself."

"Thank you. But I couldn't have done it without the help of the staff."

"Go home and get some rest. We'll see you on Monday for the public opening."

I gave them both a hug, grabbed my purse from my office, and stepped outside.

"Excuse me, Miss Kane," I heard a man's voice speak.

"Yes."

"I have been instructed to give you a ride home." He stood in front of the opened door of a black limousine.

"Thank you, but I don't accept rides from strangers." I turned around and began walking down the street.

"I would hardly call myself a stranger."

I stopped dead in my tracks and slowly turned my head, only to see Sebastian sticking his head out of the limo.

"I'm sorry, Mr.—" I cocked my head.

"Sebastian. Have you forgotten my name already?"

This was my chance. My chance to play it up as if I didn't remember him or that night.

"I'm sorry, but I've met so many people tonight."

He stepped out of the limo and stood a few feet in front of me with his hands tucked in his pockets. The way the light of the moon shined down on him made him even sexier than he already was. My body quivered just by looking at him and my knees buckled at his smile. He slowly walked over and stood in front of me. Removing his hand from his pocket, he lightly ran his finger along my jawline, sending me into a trance.

"Tonight wasn't the first time we met and you know it. You remember me and exactly what happened that night in London."

"I'm sorry, but I—"

"You do. There's no use in denying it, Chloe. Now, get in my limo and I will take you home. It's the least I can do to thank you for such a beautiful night together."

"Shit. Shit. Shit," my mouth spewed out.

"Excuse me?" His brow arched.

Shaking my head, I broke from the trance he had me in.

"What happened between us back in London stays in London. We were never supposed to see each other again. This is very awkward, Sebastian." I began hurrying down the street to escape him and this embarrassing moment.

"Chloe, wait." He chased after me. "Why is this awkward? I don't think it's awkward at all. And for God sakes, will you slow down?"

"Of course you don't think it's awkward. You're a guy and you're used to doing that sort of thing, but I'm not. I don't sleep with strange men. I never had until you," I nervously spoke as I hurried along and around the corner. He kept up with me and I wished he wouldn't have.

"I know you never had. I could tell. But don't think that I think any less of you. Damn it, Chloe! Stop!"

I stopped and looked at him. "What do you want, Sebastian?"

"I want to take you home."

I looked over at the brownstone. "I am home." I pointed.

"Oh. Are you lying?"

"Lying about what?"

"Living here? Are you just saying that so I'll leave?"

"No. I live here. In apartment 8B."

Shit. Why did I just tell him that? Not that he couldn't find out anyway. All he had to do was look at the names on the doorbell.

He brought his hand up to my cheek. "You're so beautiful, Chloe Kane, and I would like a repeat of what happened in London. You're trembling and I know you want it too."

I tried to find the words, but I couldn't speak. His touch paralyzed me.

"I—I—I don't think that will be possible."

"Why?" He smiled.

"Because you're seeing someone. The woman you were with at the gallery wouldn't appreciate you talking to me this way."

"I see a lot of women. She isn't anyone I see on a regular basis. I like to keep my options open for instances like this one."

I swallowed hard. "Well, I'm seeing someone."

"I don't believe you."

"I don't care if you believe me. I am."

He glared at me for a moment, almost as if he knew I was lying.

"Well then, he's a very lucky man. Have a good night, Miss Kane."

"You too, Sebastian." I nodded and walked to the door, inserted my key, and headed up the stairs.

As soon as I entered my apartment, I ran to the window and looked out as he walked down the street.

Chapter 9

Sebastian

As I climbed into the limo, Eli glanced at me.

"She's the one who's had you in such a bad state since you returned from London?"

I sighed. "Yes, she's the one. She claims she's seeing someone, but I don't believe her. I'm not worried. I'll have her in my bed again. It may take some time, but she will give herself to me. Just like she did in London."

"I have no doubt you're right." He smiled.

After arriving home, I poured some bourbon in a glass and pulled out my phone, pulling up the picture I took of her. I sat down in the wing-backed chair and stared at her. Her smile captivated me just like it did back in London. It was a smile that drew me to her. I couldn't believe that after all these months, I saw her again. Since that night, she had occupied my mind. It didn't matter who I was with, I always saw her. I dreamt about her and every time the scent of roses crossed my path, I was instantly reminded of her. This one woman, who was a stranger that I'd fucked on my last night in London, affected me in ways that no woman ever had before, and that posed a problem for me.

I sighed as I finished off my bourbon and headed to bed. Chloe Kane was a beautiful woman with a beautiful name. Now she was complete and I was going to stop at nothing to get her back into my bed. But I needed to be careful. I didn't want her to see me for who I really was. A monster with no emotion and no feeling. A man who couldn't cry and a man who thrived on control.

****

Chloe

"What do you mean, you turned him down?" Sienna yelled at me over facetime.

"I can't and I won't. Do you know who he is?" I continued walking down the street to Whole Foods.

"What do you mean? I know he's an extremely sexy man who wants you."

"He's a millionaire. No, make that a billionaire. Self-made when he was just twenty-one years old."

"And that's a problem how?" She twisted her face. "And most importantly, why?"

"Because we come from two different worlds. You know how those millionaires are."

"No. Actually, I don't. I've never known one."

Walking into Whole Foods, I grabbed a basket and propped my phone against my purse.

"Why would someone like him be interested in someone like me?"

"Maybe because you're beautiful and an incredibly sweet person and he sees that."

"How could he see that? We didn't talk. We just had sex," I spoke a little too loudly as the woman looking over the apples glanced up at me and shot me a look.

"Listen, Chloe, you're reading way too much into this guy. You don't even really know him."

"Just by him saying he wanted a repeat of London told me enough. All he's after is sex and from what I saw on the internet, he's a manwhore. Not to mention the fact that he basically admitted it to me. I've been through the ringer with guys in the past and there's no way in hell I'm getting involved with someone like that."

She sighed as she rolled her eyes. "No one said you have to get involved with him. Just have some fun and see what happens. If he's a total douchebag, don't see him anymore."

"I told him I was seeing someone, so he probably won't try to contact me."

"Of course you did, you silly girl."

"Okay. I'm hanging up now. I need to finish shopping because my parents are coming over."

"Have fun. I'll talk to you later."

As I opened the security door to my building, Mrs. Cooper came out of her apartment.

"Chloe, you had a delivery. Hold on." She went back inside.

A moment later, she walked out with a tall glass vase filled with yellow roses wrapped in clear plastic covering.

"Is it your birthday?" she asked.

"No. It isn't."

"Well, someone thinks you're pretty special. Here, let me take these up for you since your hands are full."

"Thank you, Mrs. Cooper."

Walking into my apartment, I set the bags on the kitchen counter while Mrs. Cooper set the flowers down on the table.

"Thanks again for your help."

"You're welcome, dear. Enjoy the flowers." She gave a friendly smile.

"I will." I walked her to the door.

After removing the wrapping, I pulled the small white envelope from the flowers and drew out the card.

Congratulations on a successful opening night.

You should be very proud.

I think a celebratory dinner is in order.

Sebastian

A small smile crossed my lips as I read the card, but a flutter in my belly also emerged. I expected this from Connor and Ellery, not Sebastian. He obviously didn't care that I said I was seeing someone unless he knew I was lying. *Ugh.* I set down the card and took the flowers over to the coffee table.

As I was preparing dinner, the doorbell rang. Looking at the time, I saw that my parents were early. Walking over to the door, I pushed the buzzer and let them in.

"You're ear—" I stopped mid-word as I opened the door and saw Sebastian standing there with a smile on his face.

"I'm early?" He grinned.

"Sebastian. What are you doing here?"

"Did you get the flowers I sent you?"

"Yes. Thank you."

"Well, I thought we could do dinner tonight. But from the sounds of it, it seems you're expecting someone."

Suddenly, my parents came up the stairs and my mom flashed a smile when she saw Sebastian.

"Oh. Hello." She looked him up and down before extending her hand. "I'm Ophelia and this is my husband, Larry. We're Chloe's parents."

Shit. Shit. Shit.

"Hello. Sebastian Bennett. It's nice to meet both of you." He lightly shook their hands.

"Are you joining us for dinner?" my mom asked as she made her way into my apartment.

"Uh, no. Actually, I just dropped by to say hi to Chloe and congratulate her on the success of last night's gallery opening."

"Oh. I knew you looked familiar. Please, join us."

"Yeah. Come on in." My dad smiled.

Could this be any more awkward?

"I'm sure Sebastian has plans tonight." I looked at him and narrowed my eye.

"Actually, I did have plans, but they recently got cancelled." He smiled.

"Then you must join us." My mom hooked her arm around his and led him into my apartment. "My, you're very muscular, Mr. Bennett."

"Please, just call me Sebastian."

Jesus, my parents and he do not mix. What the fuck was I going to do now?

"It smells delicious in here, Chloe. I'll set the table for you," my mom spoke.

"And I'll kick back on the couch with a beer. You have beer, right?" my dad asked.

"In the refrigerator, Dad." I sighed.

As my mom set the table, Sebastian came up from behind and placed his hands on my hips as I was standing in front of the stove. I froze.

"It does smell delicious." His hot breath swept over my skin. "What are you cooking?"

"Rigatoni with sautéed eggplant and tomatoes. My parents are vegetarians."

"Oh."

"You could have said no and walked away," I spoke through gritted teeth.

"I didn't want to."

He let go of my hips and made his way to the couch.

"So how do you know Chloe? Do you work together?" my mom asked.

A nervousness settled inside me. *Please don't say London. Please don't say London.*

"No. We don't work together. Actually, we met in London. It was pure coincidence that we ran into each other here in New York."

The spoon I was using hit the floor and my mom came into the kitchen, lightly grabbing my arm.

"Chloe, is he…?"

"Yes," I whispered. "I don't want to talk about it."

"Oh my God. Talk about the universe working in mysterious ways." She smiled.

"You must be 'Mr. Sexy,'" my dad spoke.

I literally just died at that very moment.

"Excuse me?" Sebastian said.

"Dinner's ready." I interrupted them and set the pasta on the table.

As I walked back into the kitchen, Sebastian followed behind.

"You told them we had sex?" he whispered.

"I tell them everything and how the hell did I know that you'd be having dinner with us?"

"Now this is awkward. How can I face them during dinner?"

"They're very sexual and open people. Believe me when I tell you that they aren't giving it a second thought."

"Is everything okay in there?" my mom asked.

"Yep. I'm just giving Sebastian some glasses." I handed him four glasses.

Chapter 10

Sebastian

I took the glasses from her and set them on the table. Taking a seat across from her parents, I gave them a small, embarrassed smile.

"So, what kind of work do you do?" her dad asked.

"I run my own company called Bennett Industries. I buy and sell real estate and failing businesses, turn them around, and sell them."

"Interesting. Chloe didn't tell us you were a corporate man," my dad spoke.

"That's because she didn't know. We just ran into each other last night for the first time since London and haven't really had a chance to talk."

"Ah, that's right. The two of you only had sex." Her dad nodded his head.

"Larry, you've embarrassed the poor man. Let's not bring that up again," my mom spoke.

I looked over at Chloe as she sat there with a smile on her face.

"There's no need for him to be embarrassed. Sex is a very open topic in our family." Her dad grinned at me.

"Can we eat now and stop talking about sex?" Chloe asked. "Sorry." She looked over at me.

"It's fine." I sighed.

"You look awful young to own a corporation. How old are you?" her mother asked.

It was a fair enough question. I wanted to put their minds at ease that I wasn't a pervy old man who sought out young women.

"I'm thirty. I started my company when I was twenty-one years old with the help of a friend of mine."

After we finished eating, Chloe's mother decided it was time for them to go, which pleased me. I couldn't escape their company fast enough. They were different, but nice. Still, knowing that they knew we had sex in London without even knowing each other bothered me.

"Your father and I have to get going."

"Mom, you don't have to leave already," Chloe spoke.

"We do. Thank you for dinner, sweetheart. We'll talk soon." She kissed her goodbye. "It was nice meeting you, Sebastian."

"Likewise." I smiled.

"Behave yourself." Her father winked at me. "Or don't." He held up his fist for a fist bump.

Shaking her head, Chloe closed the door and looked at me.

"And that was Ophelia and Larry. The people I call my parents." She lowered her head.

The only thing I wanted to do at that moment was take her to the bedroom, rip off all her clothes, and bury my cock deep inside her. The ache to feel her again was unbearable.

"They're a little odd, but nice." I smiled as I grabbed hold of her hand.

She lifted her head and her green eyes stared into mine. She pulled her hand away.

"I'm sure you're busy tonight, so you don't have to stay." She walked into the kitchen.

"You're right. I should get going. Can I use your bathroom before I leave?"

"Of course. It's the first door on the left."

Once I finished using the bathroom, I walked to the kitchen where she was standing over the sink, washing a pan. Placing my hands on hers in the soapy water, I whispered in her ear, "Thank you for dinner. I enjoyed it."

I felt her tremble and my cock immediately started to get hard.

"You're welcome," she spoke as her hands stilled in the water.

"Are you sure you want me to leave?" My lips kissed her ear.

"Yes," she spoke in a mere whisper.

"I don't want to." My lips traveled down the side of her neck.

"You have to." She tilted her head to the side.

"But I don't."

Lifting my hands out of the water, I slid them up her shirt and grabbed hold of her breasts. She moaned as I pulled the cups of her bra down, and my fingers played with her nipples.

"I bet your sweet pussy is dripping wet right now."

"No. It's not," she moaned as my hands kneaded her breasts and my tongue slid across her shoulder.

"I guess I'll have to see for myself."

Removing one hand from her breast, I slid it down the front of the black leggings she was wearing until I reached her wet opening.

"Ah. I was right," I whispered in her ear as I dipped my finger inside her and she threw her head back with a light moan. "I want to fuck you, Chloe Kane. Right here, right now. Do you want me to fuck you?"

"Yes," she panted as my finger explored her.

I turned her around, and our lips met and our tongues were reunited. Taking down her leggings and panties, I broke our kiss and lifted off her shirt so she stood there in nothing but her bra. Sliding my tongue down her chest to her taut torso, I lowered myself to my knees and slowly devoured her. Her fingers tangled through my hair as she thrust her hips forward, moaning in ecstasy. Her legs started to shake as her body gave way to her first orgasm of the night.

"Oh. My. God," she panted.

Licking my way up her, I smashed my mouth against hers as I picked her up and set her on the edge of the counter.

"I'm fucking you right here first." I reached into my back pocket and pulled out a condom.

"Okay," she spoke with bated breath as she lifted off my shirt.

With the edge of the condom wrapper in my mouth, I hurried and took down my pants, undid her bra, and threw it across the kitchen. Ripping open the wrapper, I removed the condom and slid it over my throbbing cock. Grabbing her hips and pulling her closer to the edge, I thrust inside her while her legs wrapped themselves tightly around my waist. Seizing her mouth with my lips, I kissed her hard, almost as hard as my cock was thrusting in and out of her. High-pitched moans escaped both of us as she reached down and placed both her hands firmly on my ass, pushing me in deeper until my entire length was buried inside her.

"Fuck, Chloe," I breathlessly spoke.

I lifted her from the counter, still buried inside her, and carried her over to the couch.

"Turn around and get on your knees," I commanded as I pulled out of her.

She did and grasped the back of the couch as I took her from behind, moving in and out of her with swift, long strokes.

"Do you like it this way?"

"Yes."

"How much?"

"Very much."

"How about when I do this?" I reached in front of her and pressed my fingers against her clit.

"YES," she squealed.

Grabbing hold of her hair, I pulled her head back.

"Give me those beautiful lips of yours."

She turned her head and our mouths met. When I nipped at her bottom lip, her moans became louder.

"Are you going to come for me, baby?"

"Yes. Yes."

"Good, because I'm ready to come with you."

I could feel her pussy swell around my cock as she was about to come. The pleasure was pure and raw and I couldn't hold back anymore.

"Sebastian," she yelled out.

One last deep thrust and I exploded. She lowered her head as she tried to regain her breath and I held tightly onto her hips as I pressed my lips against her back. Pulling out of her, I disposed of the condom, picked up the blanket she had sitting in the corner, and wrapped it around us as I sat down next to her, pulling her into me.

"That was some reunion."

"It sure was," she spoke as her finger ran across my chest.

"Tell me more about you."

"What do you want to know?" She looked up at me.

"Everything. How are you going to tell the guy you're seeing that you fucked another man?"

She laughed. "You know damn well I'm not seeing anyone."

"I know. I just wanted to hear you say it. Why don't you have a boyfriend?"

She got up from the couch. "I'll be right back."

A few moments later, she returned, wearing a black satin short robe.

"I'm going to grab us some wine before I get into that story." She smiled.

Getting up from the couch, I pulled on my underwear and my pants. When she emerged from the kitchen, she handed me a glass of wine and took a seat next to me.

"When I arrived in London, my boyfriend back in California and I had been broken up for two weeks. We had dated for nine months. He took me to a fancy restaurant, where I was sure he was going to ask me to move in with him, but instead, he told me he was gay."

"Are you serious?" I asked in shock.

"Yep. One hundred percent. But we're really close friends now. He's a great guy and besides Sienna, he's one of my best friends."

"Well, that's good that you remained friends with him. I didn't know you lived in California."

"Yeah. I actually just moved back here a couple of months ago. I worked at the other gallery that Connor and Ellery own in Los Angeles. I started out here as an intern for them and he moved me there as an assistant curator. Then, he moved me back here when he offered me the managing job at the new gallery."

"Remind me to thank him the next time I see him."

"How about you? Your parents must be very proud of your accomplishments."

I took in a sharp breath. Discussing my past wasn't an option. Not even with her.

"Of course they are. Listen, I better get going. I have to fly out to Minneapolis tomorrow for a meeting."

"On a Sunday?" she asked as she looked up at me.

Reaching down, my lips gently brushed against hers.

"Yes, on a Sunday. Unfortunately, my work is seven days a week."

She sat up and took a sip of her wine as I got up from the couch and finished getting dressed.

"Can I have your phone number?" I asked with a smile.

"Sure." She grinned as she rattled it off to me. "Can I have yours?" She stood up.

Running the back of my hand down her cheek, I spoke, "You'll have it when I either call you or text you."

"Oh, okay." She frowned.

After I kissed her lips one last time, she walked me to the door.

"Have a safe trip to Minneapolis."

"I will. I'll see you soon."

Climbing into the limo, I shut the door and stared at the brownstone as Eli drove away.

"How did it go?" he asked as he looked at me through the rearview mirror.

"It went good, really good." I continued to stare out the window.

Meeting her parents was the last thing I wanted to do. I'd never met a woman's parents before. That was totally unexpected and I wasn't sure how I felt about it. I could sense trouble where Chloe Kane was concerned; trouble for me. I could tell she was very family oriented and that didn't sit well with me.

Chapter 11

Chloe

"Morning." Sienna kissed my cheek as she strutted into my apartment. "I brought bagels."

"Morning. I tried calling you last night and you didn't answer." I frowned.

"Sorry. I was a bit tied up." She winked.

Rolling my eyes, I poured us each a cup of coffee. "Who tied you up this time?"

"Billy James." She grinned.

Shaking my head, I grabbed a plate for the bagels and set it on the table.

"I thought you weren't seeing him anymore."

"We aren't. We ran into each other at Starbucks last night and we got to talking, reminiscing about the great sex we used to have, and one thing led to another," she spoke as she took the bagels from the brown bag and walked over to the trashcan. "What the fuck, Chloe?!" she exclaimed as she held up the condom from last night.

"Put that down! You're nasty."

"You have five seconds to tell me what happened here last night and with whom. And you better not say it was with Sebastian because you specifically told me that you wouldn't and couldn't."

As I cut into my bagel, I sat there with a smile on my face.

"Five...four...three...two..."

"Okay. Sebastian just happened to show up here right before my parents did and my mom invited him to stay for dinner. They left. He stayed and we had sex."

Her jaw dropped as she took the seat across from me. "But—"

"I couldn't help it. He was so charming, sexy, and irresistible. It's those damn brown eyes."

She sighed as she bit into her bagel. "So now what?"

"I don't know. I like him. I know that much."

"Where is he? Didn't he stay the night or was he gone again before you woke up?"

"He left last night. He had to fly to Minneapolis this morning for a meeting."

"Hmm. So he got what he wanted and left? Sounds like me and that's not a good thing."

I shrugged. "He asked for my phone number, so I'm sure he'll call me later."

"Did you get his?"

"He said that I'll have it when he calls or texts me."

"And you don't think that's strange?"

"Whatever. If he wants to play games, he can. You know how I am about playing games."

"Good girl. Keep your head held high. I have a strange feeling about Mr. Bennett."

"What do you mean? You haven't even met him yet."

"I know I haven't, but something tells me he's a very complicated man."

"He can be complicated all he wants. This girl won't get tangled in his web." I smiled as I finished off my bagel.

****

Climbing out of bed, I made a cup of coffee and took it into the bathroom to start getting ready for work. Today was the official opening day of the gallery. Grabbing my phone from the nightstand, I checked it to see if maybe Sebastian had sent me a text message last night. He didn't and a small part of me was disappointed. It had been a week since our last encounter. Shrugging it off, I finished getting ready and headed out the door.

It was a busy week and one that I welcomed. New art pieces were delivered and displays were set up. As I was sitting at my desk researching some new ideas, my assistant, Gregory, stepped inside.

"Chloe, there's someone here who would like to speak to you. He's an artist."

"Send him in." I smiled.

Looking for new artists was the most exciting part of my job. As much as I loved historic art and artists, I also loved discovering the talents of individuals looking to break into the art world. If I could make that happen for someone, it made me happy.

As I got up from my desk, a young man, probably early twenties with short spikey black hair and piercings, walked in with a large black binder.

"This is Caden Rice," Gregory spoke before walking out and shutting the door.

Extending my hand to Mr. Rice, I spoke, "It's nice to meet you, Caden. I'm Chloe Kane. Please have a seat."

"Thank you, Miss Kane. It's nice to meet you. Thank you for seeing me."

"No problem and please call me Chloe. Now how can I help you?" I spoke as I took a seat behind my desk.

"I was wondering if you'd be interested in seeing some of my art? I would love to know your thoughts."

"Of course. Is that your art portfolio there?" I pointed.

"Yes." He set the black binder down in front of me. "I took a walk through the gallery and looked at all the art you have on display. But I did notice something you don't have, which I feel would be a great asset to this gallery."

"Oh? And what is that?"

"Open up my portfolio and you'll see." He smiled.

As I opened his portfolio and saw the first piece of art, I looked up at him with a grin.

"Contemporary Eroticism."

"Yes." He nodded.

"These are beautiful, Caden. Oh my." I smiled as I turned to the page with the photographs of provocative sculptures. "You sculpt as well?"

"Yes. All the ones you see there have been done in the last six months."

"Beautiful. I would love to have a display like this in the gallery. The human body and intimacy is a natural and beautiful thing."

"Exactly. The problem is I can't seem to find a gallery that will even look at my work."

"Why's that?" I cocked my head.

"Because the few galleries around that already have contemporary eroticism displayed aren't accepting anything new."

"Well, I think your work is something that should be shown, but, because of the nature, I'll have to talk to the owners first. I don't want to cross any lines. The other galleries Mr. Black owns don't have anything like this. If he's on board, we can set up a showing."

"Thank you, Chloe. Wow. I can't believe this." He placed his hands on his head.

Handing him a piece of paper and a pen, I asked for his phone number.

"I'll give Mr. Black a call and set up a meeting and then we'll go from there." I got up from my chair and extended my hand. "I'll be in touch, Caden."

"Thank you again, Chloe. Have a great day."

"You too." I smiled as I walked him out of my office.

Pulling my phone from my purse, I was stunned when I saw a text message from Sebastian.

"Dinner tonight. I will pick you up at seven o'clock."

What? He doesn't contact me for a week and then says we're having dinner? As much as I wanted to see him again, I wasn't going to let him do that to me.

"Nice to hear from you, Sebastian. Unfortunately, I have plans tonight so I won't be able to join you for dinner. Maybe another time."

After replying to his text message, I started to dial Connor when I heard his voice coming up the stairs.

"I was just about to call you." I smiled as he walked into my office with Gregory.

"Looks like I beat you to it. I had some business to do over here, so I thought I'd drop by and check on things. Did you need something?"

"I would like to talk to you about setting up a new display. I think Ellery should be in on the meeting as well."

"Okay. What kind of display?"

"Contemporary Eroticism."

His brow arched as he stared at me. "Oh. Interesting. Are there specific paintings you had in mind?"

"I spoke with an artist just a bit ago and he showed me his portfolio. His work is beautiful. I was going to go look at some of the galleries around and view their displays to see if there's any uniqueness."

"I see. Let's set up a meeting then." He pulled his phone from his pocket. "How about tomorrow around noon? Call the artist and have him meet us here. I'll have Ellery drop by and we'll discuss it."

"Noon is good. Thank you, Connor."

Chapter 12

Sebastian

I leaned back in my chair as I read Chloe's text message and got the impression there was a hint of anger in her words. Maybe not so much anger, but definitely an attitude. Did she really have plans tonight? Or was she just pissed off because I hadn't been in contact with her since our night together last week?

"Hello, Sebastian," Eli answered.

"I need you to follow Chloe after she leaves work and find out if she goes home or somewhere else. I want to know if she's lying to me."

"Will do."

Placing my phone in my pocket, I walked out of my office.

"I'm leaving the building, Mackenzie. I'll be back later."

"Okay, Mr. Bennett."

Stepping inside the gallery, I looked around and saw Chloe standing over by the Impressionist art display, holding up a painting against the wall. She looked so beautiful in her black short skirt and gray fitted sweater, which showed off her hourglass figure with perfection.

"Do you need help with that?" I asked as I walked up behind her.

When she turned her head, her narrowing eyes locked with mine. Fuck, she was making my cock go wild.

"No. What are you doing here, Sebastian?" she asked as she set the painting down.

"I was in the neighborhood and I thought I'd drop by and say hi, since you declined my dinner invitation."

"I'm sorry, but I have plans for tonight and I'm not cancelling because you want to have dinner. We'll have dinner together when I'm available," she spoke as she walked away.

"And what if I'm not available when you're available?" I followed her as she walked up the stairs.

"Then we'll have to get our calendars out and schedule a night we're both available."

"You're pissed off at me. I can tell."

"No, I'm not. Why would I be pissed?" she asked as we walked into her office.

"Because I didn't call or text you all week."

"Then you don't know me very well, Mr. Bennett." She smiled.

"No. Actually, I don't. The only real thing I know about you is how incredible you are to have sex with. That's why I want to have dinner with you. To get to know you better." I winked.

"I'm not sure if I should be flattered or not by that comment."

"Believe me, you should be."

Walking closer to her, I placed my hands on her hips and stared into her gorgeous green eyes.

"I need to kiss you."

"You need to or you want to?"

"Both. You look very sexy in that outfit." My hand left her hip and roamed up her skirt, pushing the crotch of her panties to the side. "You're wet." My tongue swept over my lips.

"Sebastian, please."

"Please what?" I whispered as my lips softly touched hers and my finger dipped inside her.

"We can't."

"I'm not going to fuck you, Chloe. I'm just going to give you an orgasm so you'll think about me when you're out tonight." My finger moved in and out of her.

"Oh God." She threw her head back and moaned as I dipped another finger inside.

My tongue trailed down the front of her neck, gliding across her soft skin. Pressing my thumb against her clit, I began to rub it in small circles, sending her body into a state of frenzy.

"That's right, baby. Come for me," I whispered as my mouth met hers.

I could feel the rapid beating of her heart against me and the soft subtle noises that escaped her as she orgasmed, satisfied my needs for now. Removing my fingers, I let go of her and placed one hand in my pocket. Before reaching the door, I turned and looked at her.

"Enjoy your evening tonight, Miss Kane." I winked as I walked out.

****

Chloe

I needed to sit down in order to catch my breath, not to mention the fact that my wobbly knees were ready to give out on me. Taking a seat behind my desk, I could still feel his touch.

"Are you okay, Chloe?" Gregory asked as he stepped inside my office.

"Oh yeah. I'm—I'm good." My lips gave way to a smile.

"Here are the invoices from the last shipment."

"Thank you. If everything is under control here, I'm going to a couple of art galleries and then I'm heading home."

"Enjoy the rest of your day, Chloe." He smiled. "We'll call you if anything comes up."

Getting up from my seat, I grabbed my phone and purse and headed to a couple of local art galleries to check out their displays of contemporary eroticism. When I finished and made it home, I changed my clothes and hailed a cab to Porter House New York where I was meeting Sienna and Sam for dinner.

"Well, hello there, beautiful." Sam smiled as he stood up from his seat and gave me a hug. "Long time no see."

"How are you, Sam?" I gave a small grin.

"I'm great now that I'm here with two of the most beautiful women in New York." He winked.

I looked down at Sienna, whose ass was firmly planted in the chair, only to catch her narrowing eyes looking up at me. She knew something happened today. Damn her. She always knew.

"How was your day, Chloe?" she slyly asked.

"Busy. Very busy." My eyes directed themselves to Sam. "How was your flight?" I asked to distract myself from the stand I was going to be put on, having to solemnly swear to tell the whole truth and nothing but the truth. That would have to wait, since I was not discussing the events of today in front of her English boy toy.

"The flight was good. Slept most of it. Needed to make sure I got my rest in before tonight." He winked at Sienna as she gave him a small smile.

"And how long are you in New York?"

"A week. But somehow, I think a week isn't long enough with this beauty." He took hold of Sienna's hand and brought it up to his lips.

"Aw, aren't you two just so freaking adorable." I shrugged my shoulders and wrinkled my nose.

Chapter 13

Sebastian

"I don't know why you're doing this, Sebastian," Eli commented as he pulled in front of the Time Warner Center.

"What do you mean? I'm meeting Damien for dinner."

"Of all the places in New York City, you have to dine at the same restaurant that Miss Kane is dining at?"

"Pure coincidence, my friend." I smiled as I climbed out and saw Damien waiting for me in front of the building.

We took the stairs up to the third level, and when we reached the restaurant, my eyes did a quick scan for Chloe.

"How many, Mr. Bennett?" the hostess asked as she smiled at me.

"Dinner for two and I want that table right there." I pointed.

"Actually, that table is reserved for someone else."

"Well, un-reserve it." I reached into my pocket and pulled out a fifty-dollar bill, handing it to her.

She willingly took it from my hand and then looked down at her seating chart.

"It's been un-reserved. Follow me."

Shaking his head, Damien spoke, "What's that all about?"

"I like that table."

As we followed the small framed hostess to our table, I heard my name.

"Sebastian?"

I looked over and saw Chloe sitting down with a woman and a man.

"Chloe? What are you doing here?" I pretended to act surprised.

"Having dinner with my friends. Sebastian, this is my best friend, Sienna, and her friend, Sam."

"'Ello, mate." Sam smiled as he stood up and extended his hand to me.

"Nice to meet you, Sam. Sienna, it's a pleasure. I've heard a lot about you."

"I'm sure you have." She grinned. "It's nice to finally meet you. I was beginning to think Chloe made you up."

"Chloe, this is my friend, Damien."

"Nice to meet you." She flashed her beautiful smile.

"Well, we better sit down. Enjoy your dinner. It was nice to meet both of you and it was a pleasure seeing you again, Chloe." I smirked.

Our table was right next to theirs and I made sure my seat faced Chloe. Every once in a while, I would glance over at her, only to find her observing me. As soon as our eyes met, she would look away. She didn't lie about going out tonight. She already had dinner plans and it pleased me she told the truth.

Damien leaned across the table and whispered, "Another one of your sex toys? Why haven't I met her before?"

"No. She's the one I met in London."

Damien Walters was a good friend of mine who also happened to be the vice president of my acquisitions department. We met five years ago when the company he worked for went under and I purchased it. I was highly impressed by his credentials, and being a Harvard graduate, he had a keen sense for business.

"Oh. She's sexy as fuck," he whispered.

I shot him a look and he leaned back in his chair.

"Normally, that doesn't bother you. What's going on?"

"I'm not sure yet," I replied as I took a sip of my bourbon.

****

Chloe

I could feel his stare, even if he wasn't looking at me, and my body fluttered at the thought of what happened in my office earlier this afternoon. I hadn't stopped thinking about him since he left and to see him here tonight was bliss. Sienna knew something was up because she got up and announced to Sam that we were going to the restroom.

As we stepped inside, she lightly grabbed my arm.

"Okay. What happened to you today? And don't say nothing because you've been glowing like a firefly on a hot summer's night since you walked in here."

Setting my purse on the counter, I dug for my lipstick.

"He came into the gallery today and —"

"You had sex with him in the gallery?!" she shrieked.

I looked under the stalls to make sure nobody else overheard her mouth.

"Keep it down. No. Not really." I smiled.

"What do you mean 'not really'?"

"He just made me orgasm and then he left."

The shocked expression that overtook her face made me laugh.

"What do you mean he made you orgasm? You said you didn't have sex."

I held up my index finger.

"Oh," she let out in a long drawl with wide eyes.

"He texted me and asked me to dinner. I declined because I was meeting you and Sam, so he came to the gallery and told me he wanted to give me something so I would think about him tonight."

"Fuck! That is so hot! I need a man like that." She pouted.

"You have Sam for the next week."

She rolled her eyes. "I know. Somehow, I don't think he'll be a Sebastian."

"You'll survive." I smiled as I put my lipstick in my purse. "I have to pee. I'll meet you back at the table."

After washing my hands, I dried them off, and when I opened the bathroom door, I found Sebastian leaning up against the wall with his hands pushed in his pockets.

"Hi." I smiled.

"Is anyone else in there?" he asked.

"Umm. No. It was just me."

Next thing I knew, his mouth was on mine as he pushed me back into the bathroom, his hands planted firmly on each side of my face.

"Are you going straight home after here?" he asked as he broke our kiss.

"Yes."

"Good. I'll be over after I finish dinner. We have some unfinished business from this afternoon."

His eyes stared into mine as he kissed my lips one last time before leaving the bathroom. I stood there frozen as I tried to process what just happened, my heart beating rapidly and an ache down below that was screaming with desire.

When I arrived home, I kicked off my shoes and went to the bedroom to strip out of my clothes and put on my satin robe. When he got here, there would be no time wasted, but somehow, I had a feeling it was going to be a fuck and leave, something I didn't want. I wanted to fall asleep with his strong arms wrapped tightly around me while my head lay on his muscular chest.

The door buzzer rang and I let him up. I stood in the doorway in my robe, and he smiled as he brushed his lips against mine and kicked the door shut with his foot. He wasted no time untying my robe and sliding it off my shoulders.

"Fuck, Chloe," he growled as his eyes raked over my naked body.

Taking off his suit coat, he unbuttoned his shirt and threw it to the ground, along with his shoes and pants. Grabbing my arms, he pushed me up against the bare wall that sat opposite of the kitchen. His urgency to fuck me could no longer be contained and his determination to take me against the wall heightened my arousal. His lips caressed my neck as his fingers plunged inside me. I gasped and a low moan escaped deep within his chest.

"Are you on birth control?"

"Yes," I replied breathlessly.

"What kind?"

"The pill. Why?"

"I don't want to wear a condom tonight." His pleading brown eyes locked on mine.

Our mouths met and a sensation of warmth engulfed me. I wrapped my legs around his waist and placed my hand on the back of his neck while he thrust inside me with deep, long strokes as his arms held me up effortlessly. I panted as he moved in and out of me, digging my nails into the back of his neck as the wave of an orgasm came in and swept me away. He moaned as sweat dripped from his forehead.

"Turn around, baby, and face the wall," he commanded as he unwrapped my legs from his waist.

I did as he asked; his hands latched onto my breasts and his tongue slid up and down my spine before he thrust into me from behind. Letting go of my breasts, he placed his hands against the wall and rapidly moved in and out of me, letting soft whispers of ecstasy escape his lips. One last deep thrust and he slowed down, filling me up with his come. He placed one arm around my waist and gently lowered us to the ground. We lay there, his heart beating fiercely against my back as his lips pressed against my shoulder. My hand wrapped around his arm, never wanting him to let go. I could feel his cock soften and he pulled out of me.

"How was your dinner?" he asked.

I turned my head and looked at him. Smiling, I spoke, "It was good. How was yours?"

"Perfection now that I've had my dessert."

He got up from the floor and held his hand out to me. After helping me up, he picked my robe up from the floor and slipped it over my shoulders as he kissed my lips.

"I have to get going. I have an early meeting tomorrow morning."

Disappointment shot through me, killing my extremely good mood.

"I want you to stay the night."

"And I want to, but I can't. You understand, right?" He cupped my chin in his hand.

"Yeah. I understand."

"Good. I knew you would."

I watched him as he got dressed and then I walked him to the door.

"I'll be in touch. Thank you for a beautiful evening." He smiled as he kissed my forehead and then my lips.

Shutting the door, I stood there and stared at it as thoughts escalated in my head. Thoughts of Sebastian, the mind-blowing sex we had, and the way he always left after. The only night he stayed was in London and that was because it was his hotel room, but he was sure as shit gone the next morning. Concerns filled my mind at the possibility of him using me for his own sexual pleasure. It was too late for me. My attachment to him wasn't only physical, for now the emotional attachment settled in, leaving me feeling rejected and used.

Chapter 14

Chloe

After taking a shower, I climbed into bed and facetimed Sienna. I knew she probably wouldn't answer because she was with Sam, but it was worth a shot. I desperately needed to talk to her.

"Hello, gorgeous." Her smiling face appeared on the screen. She was covered in a sheet, lying in bed.

"I'm not interrupting anything, am I?"

"Not at the moment. What's up?"

I sighed. "Sebastian came over and, once again, it was a wham bam, thank you ma'am."

"What was his excuse this time?" She rolled her eyes.

"He has an early meeting in the morning."

"He is a corporate hot shot and I'm sure he does. The least he could have done was bring an extra pair of clothes with him. What's that look for?"

"What look?"

"Please don't tell me you've become emotionally attached."

"Who's emotionally attached?" I heard Sam say as Sienna turned her phone and his naked body appeared on the screen as he walked by.

"Gah. Stop that!"

"Doesn't he have the cutest little ass?" Sienna smiled. "Anyway, back to your emotional attachment. Don't let him use you like that. You're one of the strongest women I know. Don't let his good looks and great sex take advantage of you. The next time he wants sex, you ask him if he's hitting the road after. If he says yes, kick him out the door."

"Good advice, S. Hey, Chloe." Sam waved.

"Hey, Sam."

"We'll talk more about this tomorrow. Get some sleep and try not to think about him, okay?"

"Okay."

Well, she was no help. As I pulled the covers over me and sank into my bed, I couldn't stop thinking about how I knew nothing about Sebastian Bennett. All I knew was that he owned his own multi-billion-dollar company. He didn't seem to want to share anything about himself, or maybe because the opportunity wasn't there. Every time we were together, it consisted of nothing but sex, and then he left. My one night with a stranger in a foreign country turned out to be many nights with a stranger in America, and that was exactly what he was: a stranger. Just because I knew his name, job, and age didn't mean I really knew him at all.

The next morning, I stumbled out of bed, showered, and headed to the gallery. After a busy morning, I glanced at the clock. It was almost noon.

"I'm going to head up to my office," I spoke to Gregory and Micha. "Connor, Ellery, and Caden should be here shortly."

As I sat down at my desk, I picked up my phone to see if I had any messages. None. Zero. Zilch. Somewhere in the back of my dumb head, the thought that Sebastian might have sent me a text message to at least say "hi" came forth. As I set my phone down, I saw Connor and Ellery walk in.

"Good afternoon." Ellery smiled as she walked over and gave me a hug. "Is he here yet? I'm dying to see his work." Her grin widened.

"Not yet."

"Why don't we go out there and wait for him?" Connor spoke as he walked over to the couch and took a seat.

I could hear Gregory's voice coming up the stairs. Looking over, I saw Caden.

"Connor, Ellery, this is Caden. Caden, these are the owners of the gallery, Connor and Ellery Black."

"Nice to meet you." Ellery smiled as she extended her hand.

After hellos were said, we all took seats in the area outside my office and Caden opened up his portfolio. I studied Ellery's face as she previewed the artist's work. I could tell she loved it. Then I looked over at Connor as he cleared his throat.

"Well, I must say these are—" He took in a sharp breath. "Very artistic."

I couldn't help but let out a light laugh.

"Ellery?" he asked.

"I love it and I think it's a great idea to hold a month-long exhibition. This gallery is perfect the way it is, but adding a little sex to it would make it even better."

I watched Connor as he swallowed hard. "Chloe?" He glanced at me.

"I think it's beautiful work and we should go with it."

"I've added some framed black and white photographs towards the end. Not only do people like the realism of my paintings, but they like the still photography I do as well."

"Beautiful," Ellery and I spoke at the same time as we stared at the photos.

"Indeed it is." Connor smiled.

Ellery glared at him and lightly smacked his arm.

"What? They are beautiful photographs. I'm agreeing with you. Caden, this gallery would love to exhibit your artwork. Chloe will handle everything and go over with you how we handle commissions and sales."

Caden's face lit up as he thanked Connor and Ellery. We said our goodbyes and I took Caden into my office.

"We'll set up the exhibition in two weeks. That'll give us enough time to advertise, invite, and get your work in here." I reached in my desk drawer and pulled out a contract. "Here is the contract for your art. Read it over, and if you agree with everything, sign it and return it to me when you deliver your paintings. Also, I want to set up a few sculptures, so make sure you send them as well."

"I can't even believe this. Thank you so much, Chloe. I owe you big time."

"You're welcome and you don't owe me anything. I'm just doing my job." I smiled.

I walked him out of the gallery and turned my attention to Gregory.

"I need you to run an ad for the exhibition and send out some invites."

"Where are we going to put the display?" he asked.

"Second level. We have all that space up there on the other side of my office. We're going to need some more display cubes and a sign to put down here indicating that Contemporary Eroticism is upstairs. Have Micha take care of that."

"Will do, Chloe."

"Thanks. I'm heading out to lunch now, so I'll be back."

As I was walking out the gallery doors, Sebastian stopped me.

"Going somewhere?" He smiled.

"Lunch." My belly fluttered at the sight of him.

"Perfect timing. Me too." He held out his arm.

What the hell. I placed my arm in his and we walked down the street to a small but cozy Italian restaurant.

****

Sebastian

I wasn't going to see her today. In fact, I had planned on not calling her or seeing her for about a week. She consumed my mind every waking minute and I even found myself dreaming about her when I slept. This wasn't supposed to happen. It never had with any other woman and this concerned me a great deal that it happened with her. No matter how hard I tried to put Chloe Kane out of my mind, she wouldn't leave.

"I had a wonderful time with you last night." I smiled as I reached across the table and placed my hand on hers.

"Me too. But it would have been better if you had stayed the night."

"I'm sorry about that, but I couldn't. I told you I had an early meeting this morning."

"I know. I was just saying that it would have been better." She took a sip from her wine glass.

I was about to do something that I had never done before.

"How would you like to go away with me for the weekend?"

"Where?" She smiled.

"Vegas. I have a business meeting. It won't take long and then we can have the rest of the weekend together to do whatever you want."

"You mean we can actually sleep together in a bed?" She smirked.

"That and many other things." I winked.

She bit down on her bottom lip. "When are you leaving?"

"Tomorrow."

"I have to work all day."

I pulled my phone from my pocket and dialed Connor.

"Connor Black," he answered.

"Connor, it's Sebastian."

"Hello, Sebastian. To what do I owe the pleasure?"

"Would you mind if I stole Chloe Kane tomorrow?"

"What do you mean?"

"I'm flying to Vegas and I would like her to go with me, but she says she has to work."

"Oh. I didn't know the two of you were seeing each other."

"That's yet to be determined."

"Ah, I see. If she can swing the day off, it's fine with me. She's the manager and she knows if she can or can't."

"Thank you, my friend. I'll be in touch."

"Sebastian, wait. Chloe is a great woman and I know I don't have to—"

"I know and, no, you don't."

"Okay. Have fun in Vegas."

"Thanks. We'll talk soon."

Chloe sat across from me with wide eyes as she listened to me talk to her boss. I knew Connor wouldn't mind, but I needed to put Chloe's mind at ease.

"I cannot believe you just called him."

"Why? We're friends. He said that he doesn't have a problem with you taking the day off as long as you feel you can. So can you?"

"I don't know. I have an exhibition coming up in a couple of weeks."

"Then you can work extra hard on Monday." I smiled.

"Fine. I'll go to Vegas with you."

"Excellent. I'll pick you up tomorrow morning at eight a.m."

"What time does our flight leave?"

"Whenever I want it to."

She narrowed her eye at me as if she didn't understand.

"I have my own private jet, Chloe."

"Really?" She smiled. "That is so cool."

I chuckled. "I'm happy you think it's cool." I looked at my watch. "If we're finished here, I must get back to the office."

"And I must get back to the gallery."

I paid the bill and placed my hand on Chloe's back as we exited the restaurant. Walking her back to the gallery, I softly kissed her lips.

"I'll see you tomorrow morning."

"Thank you for lunch."

"You're welcome." I pushed a strand of her beautiful blonde hair behind her ear.

I climbed into the limo and sank back against the lush black leather. What the fuck was I doing?

Chapter 15

Chloe

As I walked into the gallery, I was on cloud nine.

"Gregory, Micha, I won't be in tomorrow, so I'll need you both to handle things while I'm gone." I grinned.

"No worries, Chloe."

I stood there with a twisted face, waiting for one of them to ask me why I was taking the day off. They didn't.

"Aren't you going to ask why I won't be here?" I placed my hands on my hips and cocked my head.

They looked at each other.

"It really isn't our business why you take the day off," Gregory spoke.

"Well, I'm making it your business. Go ahead. Ask me."

"Why won't you be in tomorrow?" Micha asked.

"Because I'm going to Vegas for the weekend!" I exclaimed with excitement.

"How fun!" Gregory spoke. "Who are you going with?"

"Mr. Sebastian Bennett."

"Lucky girl," Micha replied. "He's dreamy."

"He sure is. If you'll excuse me, I have some work I want to finish before I leave."

I couldn't believe Sebastian asked me to go away with him. Two nights and three days of us having nothing but sex, sex, and more sex, not to mention the fact that I would be snuggled up against him all night long, feeling his warm naked body pressed against mine and his strong arms wrapped tightly around me. I needed to call Sienna.

"Hello, friend." Her face appeared on the screen as she sat at her desk.

"Guess who's leaving for Vegas tomorrow morning?"

"I don't know. Your parents?"

"No, silly girl. Me! Sebastian asked me to go with him and I said yes. So I will be unavailable starting tomorrow through Sunday."

"The man is wising up. I'm so happy for you."

"This could really be the start of something, Sienna. I'm totally crazy about him."

"Listen, Chloe, and don't take this the wrong way. You know I love you, but for the love of God, don't get yourself caught up in him. I don't want you to get hurt. I have never seen you react like this to a guy before and, to be honest, it's scaring me."

I rolled my eyes at her.

"Don't roll your eyes at me. You know it's true. I'm just looking out for your well-being."

"And I appreciate that, but this is all your fault."

"How the hell is it my fault?" She frowned.

"You're the one who pushed me into having a one-night stand with a stranger in a foreign country. Had you never done that in that first place, I never would have thought about it and acted on it. Hence this being all your fault." I smiled.

"Oh my God! You're so good." She laughed. "I have to go, darling. Sam just walked in and we're going to lunch. Say hi to Chloe." She turned the phone so I could see him.

"Hello there, gorgeous." He smiled as he waved.

"Hey, Sam. Enjoy lunch and I'll talk to you later, Sienna."

"Have fun in Vegas and I want all the juicy details when you get back. Or feel free to face time me while you're in bed. I'd love to see him naked." She winked.

After ending the call, I finished the work I was going to do tomorrow and headed home to pack a bag.

****

When the bellhop unlocked the door to the suite, I gulped as I stepped inside of the Italian marble foyer. Sebastian walked past and then stopped and looked at me as I stood there frozen.

"What's wrong?" He chuckled.

"This is so beautiful."

115

"Please step inside to the main area. If you think the foyer is beautiful, wait until you see the rest." He held out his hand.

Placing my hand in his, he escorted me into the living room.

"Wow. Seriously?" I smiled.

"Seriously." He winked.

"How big is this suite?"

"Approximately two thousand square feet."

I was surrounded by Italian marble, furnishings, and décor. The room was impeccably decorated and the artwork on the walls spoke for itself.

"Would you like to see the bedroom?" Sebastian asked.

"Of course. I'm sure it's bigger than my apartment."

He narrowed his eye at me for a moment. "Yeah. I think it is."

In the bedroom, I crawled across the luxurious extra-large king-sized bed.

"Oh my God, this is so comfortable. I'm going to sleep like a baby." I sprawled out on my back.

"Hate to break the news to you, sweetheart, but you won't be getting very much sleep."

"Okay." I grinned as I propped myself up on my elbows.

He gave me a smile and then looked at his watch. Stepping towards the bed, he leaned over and kissed me.

"As much as I want to fuck you in this bed, right now, I have that meeting to get to. I shouldn't be more than a couple of hours. You can stay here in the room or go check out the hotel, but whatever you do, don't leave. I don't want you wandering around Vegas by yourself. Deal?"

"Deal."

"There will be plenty of time for everything else over the next couple of days," he growled.

Standing up, he pulled a money clip from his pocket that held a ridiculous wad of cash.

"Here. Take this in case you want to go down to the casino. They have some nice slot machines."

"You don't have to give me money. I have my own."

"Take it, Chloe." He arched his brow.

"If you insist." I smiled as I took it from him.

Kissing me one last time, he walked out and went to his meeting. I'd never been in such a luxurious place in my entire life. The entire suite was simply breathtaking. The marble bathroom had an oval-shaped jet tub and an enormous glass-encased separate shower. There was a media room off the living area, which featured a built in wall HD TV and a cream-colored sectional that surrounded the room.

Holding the money that Sebastian gave me in my hand, I counted it.

"Holy mother of pearl," I said out load. He had given me a thousand dollars.

Making my way down to the casino, I took a seat at the blackjack table. As I was sitting there with a crowd gathered around me, I felt a tap on my shoulder. When I turned my head, I saw Sebastian standing there.

"Hey. Is your meeting over already?"

"Already? It's been four hours. I sent you numerous text messages and you didn't respond," he spoke with a hint of anger.

"Wow. Really? I've been sitting here for four hours?" I bit down on my bottom lip. "This is my last hand."

"What the hell, Chloe? How much did you win?"

"I don't know." I shrugged as the dealer dealt the final card and I won. "Woohoo!" I held my hands up in the air. "Thanks, Chuck. It's been fun, but I have to go."

"Congratulations, Chloe." He smiled.

I gathered up all my chips, put them in a large cup, and handed it to Sebastian.

"Here you go." I grinned.

"What are you doing?" He looked down at the chips.

"It's yours. You can thank me later." I patted his chest and started to walk away.

"Hold on a second. If I'm seeing these chips right, there has to be over five thousand dollars here."

"Give or take a couple of hundred."

"How the hell did you win this?"

"The sun is in Leo right now." I smiled.

"What?" He frowned.

"Forget it. I was just lucky tonight. That's all."

After cashing in the chips, we went up to the suite.

"Take this," he spoke as he handed me the money.

"No. It's yours. You gave me money to play and I won. So I'm giving it back."

"Fine. I'll take back the thousand dollars I gave you and you keep the rest."

"Seriously, Sebastian. Keep it. It was your money that won."

Chapter 16

Sebastian

I couldn't believe I was standing there arguing with her over the money that she won. Most importantly, I couldn't believe she was refusing to take four thousand dollars. Who the fuck does that? Not any woman I'd ever known. If I had chosen to give any of the women I had been with that kind of money, they'd snatch it from my hand and run to the nearest designer store. But Chloe was different from anyone I'd ever known and I couldn't explain why. I had felt it the night I fucked her for the first time in London. The innocence that radiated from her was pure.

"I'm not arguing with you about this. You are taking the money that you won. End of discussion. Go buy something nice with it. Maybe a painting you love and think of me every time you look at it." I smiled as I ran my hand down her cheek.

"Fine. If it'll shut you up, I'll keep it."

Arching my brow at her, I spoke, "If it'll shut me up? I can think of something right now that will shut me up but make you scream."

"And what's that?" The corners of her mouth curved up.

"Oh, I think you know." My hand slid up the short sundress she was wearing and cupped her.

She let out a light moan.

"But maybe we should eat first." I removed my hand and walked away, grinning from ear to ear.

"I—I don't want to eat right now," she muttered.

"Then what do you want, Chloe?" I asked as I turned around and stood a few feet away from her.

"You. We can eat later."

"So instead of eating dinner, you want me to fuck you?" My cock was already standing at full force.

"Yes." A small smile crossed her lips.

"Is your pussy wet?"

"Yes."

I already knew she was wet. I felt the deliciousness through her panties.

"Maybe you need to feel for yourself just to be sure."

As I stood there, I watched her as she took down the straps of her sundress, letting it fall to the ground. My God, she was perfect. Placing her hand down the front of her panties, she felt herself and my cock was already set to explode. Many women had touched themselves for me, but when she did it, it took my breath away.

"I'm very wet." She continued to play with herself.

I swallowed hard because I couldn't hold back. This wasn't going to be nice and slow. It was going to be rough and hard because that was what she did to me. I quickly unbuttoned my shirt and took it off. As I unbuttoned my pants, I slowly walked towards her. She took down her panties and placed her fingers on her clit, sensually rubbing herself with a seductive look on her face.

"Do you have any idea what you're doing to me?" I growled as I pulled down and stepped out of my pants.

She didn't say a word as she stared at me. Wrapping one arm around her, I took her down on the ground, moving her hand away so I could finish the job. Stimulating her was gratifying and I could do it all night. She lay on the floor, safe in my arms as my fingers moved in and out of her. As much as I wanted to kiss her soft lips, I resisted because I wanted to watch the expression on her face when she came.

"Are you going to come?" I asked.

"Yes. Oh God yes!" she moaned as her body tightened.

Closing her eyes and with her lips parted, she let out a low groan as I felt the warmth pour from her. Her sounds were music to my ears.

"I need you now!" I climbed on top of her and thrust deep inside.

Wrapping her legs around me, her hips moved in sync. Her pussy was so hot that it was taking everything I had not to blow so soon. I needed to control myself, so I slowed down and took in the beautiful eyes that stared back at me as I slowly moved in and out of her.

"Is this what you wanted?" I smiled as I pushed a strand of hair from her forehead.

"Yes." She smiled. "Now isn't this much better than eating?"

"It sure is, sweetheart." I kissed her lips and picked up the pace.

After a few hard thrusts, my cock, which was more than ready, exploded inside her.

****

Chloe

As he lowered his body onto mine, we lay there in an embrace, my fingers deftly running up and down his back. I was more than satisfied, at least for the time being.

"Shall we eat now?" I asked.

He lifted his head and, with a smile, he spoke, "Yes. We shall. I'm starving."

He climbed off of me and helped me up.

"Are we going out or staying in?" I asked.

"Which do you prefer?"

"It doesn't matter. I'm good with either."

He walked into the bedroom and pulled a pair of sweatpants from his suitcase. I followed behind, grabbing the white robe from the closet.

"How about we enjoy a nice evening in, and then we can spend the whole day tomorrow exploring Vegas?" he spoke.

"I like that idea." I pulled my phone from my purse. "Oh, look at that. Some guy named Sebastian sent me like ten text messages."

"You should have responded and then I wouldn't have had to send so many."

He walked over to the desk and grabbed the in-room dining menu from it. He took it to the couch, and I followed and sat down next to him.

"I didn't hear my phone. I was too busy winning all that money." I grinned.

"I figured you were at the casino, but I was still worried."

Hearing him say he was worried struck something inside. "I can take care of myself."

"I'm sure you can. But still, you should check your phone every once in a while. And by the way, what exactly did you mean by 'the sun is in Leo'?"

"It's an astrological thing. If you don't follow it, you wouldn't understand."

"You follow that stuff?"

"Yep. In case you didn't notice, my parents are throwbacks from the sixties. They are very spiritual, astrological, open people. I was brought up on it."

He chuckled. "I bet they smoke weed too." He looked at the menu.

"They do," I spoke with seriousness. "And hearing you say 'weed' just killed me."

"Why?"

"Because you're so proper and formal. I was expecting you to use another word, like cannabis."

He cocked his head as his eyes stared into mine. "Do they really smoke cannabis?"

"Yes. So if you're over at their house some time, don't be offended when Larry pulls it out and starts smoking it. I'm just putting you on alert now." I smiled.

"Thanks for the heads up. Now, do you like filet? Because I noticed you aren't a vegetarian."

"I love filet."

"Cooked how?"

"Medium rare."

"Ah. A girl after my own heart. I don't know too many women who eat their steak like that."

"I bet you know a lot of women," I blurted out.

"Yes. I do." He smirked.

"And I bet you've been with a lot of women." My mouth wouldn't stop.

He glared at me for a moment. "Yes. I have." His eye narrowed at me.

"And you never found anyone special?" I cocked my head.

"No. What's with all the questions?"

"Nothing. I'm just surprised someone as confident, sexy, and rich as you, hasn't latched on to someone."

He got up from the couch and walked over to the phone.

"First of all, I don't latch on to anyone. Second of all, relationships are off the table."

Ouch. Double ouch. Triple ouch. I felt that knife stabbing my heart.

"Why?"

"Because. Now I have to call our order in. So please, no more questions."

After he finished placing the order, he walked over to the bar and opened the bottle of Prosecco the hotel generously provided upon our arrival.

"Thank you," I spoke as he handed me a glass.

His mood had suddenly changed. Apparently, the talk of relationships was taboo. Was saying that relationships were off the table a hint to me? Was he making himself clear that whatever it was we were doing was never going to amount to anything else? I was going to forget what he said for now and enjoy the rest of our time in Vegas.

Chapter 17

Sebastian

I knew it wouldn't be long before the questions were asked. What the hell was I thinking bringing her to Vegas? I knew it was a risk, but at the time, I didn't care. As we lay in bed after another round of sex, Chloe decided she was going to take a bath.

"Would you like to join me?" she asked.

"No. You go ahead. I'm just going to go over some notes from the meeting."

"Okay." She smiled as she kissed me.

Watching her get out of bed and walk to the bathroom completely naked was heart-stopping. Her body was pure perfection and it was what I most desired. An unexplainable desire. Dinner was quiet. My mood had changed the minute she brought up other women, a topic that I was never going to discuss with her.

As I was flipping through my notes, I heard her softly singing in the bathtub. I couldn't help but smile at the distraction, so I climbed out of bed and walked into the bathroom.

"You have a beautiful singing voice." I smiled as I stood next to the tub.

"Thanks. Have you changed your mind about joining me?"

I stood there for a moment and took in the beautiful sight in front of me.

"Yeah. I have."

She sat up and moved towards the front while I climbed in behind her. As I wrapped my arms around her, she snuggled against me.

"What does your father do for a living?" I asked.

"He's a street performer slash club singer."

"Huh?" I tilted my head.

"By day, he plays his guitar and sings around the city and, by night, he performs in clubs."

"What kind of music does he play?"

"Folk mostly."

"And your mother?"

"She's a spiritual advisor and she teaches yoga."

"A what?" I asked in confusion.

"A spiritual advisor." She turned her head and looked at me.

"Oh. Yeah. A spiritual advisor. I didn't hear you correctly the first time."

To me, that was odd.

"What about your parents?" she innocently asked.

I knew what was at risk when I asked her about her parents.

"My parents have been dead for many years, and I'll be honest with you, Chloe, I don't want to talk about them," I spoke in an authoritative voice.

"Okay. I'm sorry." She removed my arms from her and climbed out of the tub.

"Where are you going?"

"I really don't feel like taking a bath anymore. I'm tired and I think I'm just going to go to sleep. You wore me out, Mr. Bennett."

I hurt her feelings. Climbing out of the tub, I wrapped a towel around my waist and walked into the bedroom where Chloe was putting on her nightgown. Walking up behind her, I wrapped my arms around her waist and pressed my lips against her shoulder.

"Hey, I'm sorry if I sounded abrupt. It's just a sensitive subject and it's something I don't like to talk about. I need you to respect that."

"It's fine, Sebastian. I didn't know."

"I know you didn't," I whispered. "Let's go to bed. We have a big day tomorrow touring the city. I thought maybe you'd like to go see Cirque du Soleil tomorrow night."

"I've heard really good things about that show. Isn't it sold out?" she asked as she turned around in my arms.

Flashing her a smile, I spoke, "I have a couple of tickets."

"Sounds like fun. I would love to go see that."

I kissed her forehead, and we climbed into bed. As we lay there, our bodies meshed tightly against one another and it reminded me of our one night in London. The night that I so freely held her while she slept. Another thing I didn't understand. The overwhelming need to want to hold her. I never held the women I slept with. After fucking them, I either left or turned on my side to face the other way. The one thing I always stayed true to was that I would leave before they awoke. Now that we got the whole parents thing out of the way, hopefully, the questions about my past would stop. But somehow, I doubted it.

I opened my eyes and smiled when I saw Chloe staring up at me.

"Good morning." I kissed the top of her head.

"Good morning."

"How long have you been awake?" I asked.

"Just a few minutes. I didn't want to wake you, so I didn't move."

I tightened my grip around her. "I'm happy you didn't."

She wiggled out of my grip and sat up. "I'm starving. That last round of sex in the middle of the night ravaged me."

I chuckled. She was lying on her side with her back to me and when I woke up in the middle of the night, and I couldn't help myself.

We spent the day shopping, eating, going into a couple of art galleries, and then we decided to sit by the pool for a while and sip a few cocktails before getting ready to go to Cirque du Soleil. Seeing Chloe naked was one thing, but seeing her in the bikini she wore made my cock go crazy. Crazy enough that as soon as we got back to the room, we barely made it through the door before her bottoms were off and I was thrusting deep inside her.

****

Chloe

As Sebastian and I were dressing for the show, my phone rang, and Sienna popped up on the screen.

"Hi there," I answered with a grin.

"My, my. Look at you in that sexy red dress. Where are you off to?"

"Cirque du Soleil."

"Lucky bitch. I've always wanted to see that. Is he around?"

"Yeah. He's in the bedroom getting dressed."

"Oh? Turn the phone around so I can have a peek."

"No." I laughed.

Sebastian walked into the bathroom in just his dress pants and I thought Sienna was going to go into cardiac arrest.

"Good God."

"Sebastian, say hi to Sienna."

"Hi, Sienna." He smiled as he waved.

"Hello there, Mr. Bennett," she spoke in her seductive voice.

Rolling my eyes, I took my phone to the living room.

"Jesus, Chloe. That man is a god."

"You don't have to tell me twice."

"Okay. Go have fun. I just wanted to tell you really quick that Sam has decided to stay another week."

"Really? Why?" I frowned.

"Because he doesn't want to leave me." She winked.

"But do you want him around for another week?"

She shrugged. "He's fun and—" She paused.

"And what? My eye narrowed at her.

"He's fun. Ta ta, love. See you soon."

She ended the call before I could say something. Shaking my head, I set my phone down and walked into the bedroom to put on my shoes.

"You look simply stunning," Sebastian spoke as he ran his fingers across my shoulder and swept his lips over my neck.

"Thank you, and so do you." I smiled.

Cirque du Soleil was beyond fantastic. After the show, Sebastian suggested we do some gambling.

"How about we hit the casinos for a while?"

"I don't think that's a good idea."

"Why not? The sun is in Leo." He smirked.

"Actually, it's not anymore. We're at the start of the Venus retrograde. It's not wise to gamble or invest in anything during this phase."

He looked at me like I was crazy.

"And you believe all that?" he asked as he cocked his head.

"Yes."

"Well, I'll take my chances."

"Okay. Don't say I didn't warn you. I'll just watch."

We headed back to the Palazzo and straight into the casino.

"I think I'll hit the high roller room." He smiled.

"Oh. I wouldn't do that. Why don't you just stick to the normal piss poor people tables?"

He chuckled. "Fine. I'll start there and move to the high roller room later."

Sebastian took a seat at the blackjack table where Chuck from last night was the dealer.

"Hey. Welcome back, Chloe." He smiled.

"Hi, Chuck."

"Aren't you playing tonight?"

"No." I shook my head. "We're in a Venus retrograde right now. Not a lucky night." I winked.

Sebastian turned his head and looked at me.

"Do you really have to tell people that?" he asked in an irritated way.

I didn't respond. I just gave him a small smile.

"Ah. I see," Chuck spoke.

After about ten hands, Sebastian was down a lot of money. After his last losing game, he decided it was time to get up from the blackjack table and head somewhere else.

"Apparently, blackjack isn't a good game to play tonight. I think I'll try my luck at roulette."

"You're going to play the Devil's game?" I frowned.

He stopped walking and stared at me.

"What do you mean?"

"Hello. All the numbers on the wheel add up to 666. The Devil's number."

"Don't be ridiculous, Chloe." He laughed.

He wasn't laughing anymore when he lost over and over again. He was starting to become irritated. I could see it in his face. We left the roulette table and walked into the elegant poker room that was designated for people of Sebastian's status.

"Fuck this," he spoke in an irate voice as we walked out three hours later.

"Told ya. Venus retrograde."

"Save it, Chloe." He walked a couple steps in front of me.

When we entered the room, he immediately took off his suit coat and threw it across the wing-backed chair in the living room. Pouring himself a drink, he stood in front of the window and stared out into the brightly lit, busy city. He was pissed he lost all that money, but I warned him. Now it was up to me to make him feel better and to forget about the money he lost. Placing my iPhone in the docking station, I pulled up my playlist and the song *American Idiot* by Green Day started to play. I danced over to where Sebastian was standing, moving all around him as he stood there and stared at me. Bringing my hands in the air, I shimmied my body around, dancing across the suite and singing as loud as I could. Finally, he cracked a smile as he stood there and shook his head. As the song was ending, there was a loud knock at the door. I turned the music off and Sebastian walked over to the door.

"Excuse me, Mr. Bennett. I'm sorry to disturb you, but we had some complaints about music being played too loudly up here."

Sebastian sighed as he looked at me.

"I'm sorry. It won't happen again."

"Very well, sir. Enjoy the rest of your evening."

"How are we supposed to enjoy our evening if we can't play a little loud music," I shouted from across the room.

Sebastian shut the door and turned to me.

"Now you've got us in trouble."

"Oh please." I waved my hand. "By the way, don't ever tell my parents I have that song on my playlist. They would be so pissed."

He chuckled as he walked over to me and picked me up. Wrapping my arms around his neck, I stared into his mysterious brown eyes.

"What are you doing?"

"Taking you into the bedroom and fucking you. That little dance of yours seemed to have turned me on."

"Ah." I grinned. "I can dance on the bed if you'd like."

"Only if you promise to do it naked." A smile crossed his lips.

"I think I can do that."

He carried me into the bedroom, where we made love for hours.

Chapter 18

Chloe

Sebastian carried my bag for me to my apartment.

"Home sweet home," I spoke as I stepped inside.

"You've only been gone a couple of days." He laughed.

"I know, but I like my apartment and it's good to be back. Speaking of which, I have no clue where you even live." I pressed my finger against his chest.

"I live in a penthouse on Park Avenue."

"Of course you do." I smiled as I took my bag from him.

"What's that supposed to mean?" he asked as he followed me to the bedroom.

"Nothing. You're rich and rich people live in stuffy penthouses."

"It's not stuffy. It happens to be very comfortable."

"I'm sure it is with your beige walls, dark trim, and dark hardwood floors."

He stood there and stared at me like he was going to say something but didn't. Walking over to me, he placed his hands on my hips and kissed my forehead.

"I have to go. I'll have you over to my stuffy penthouse one day." He smiled.

"Okay."

"I'll be in touch. Have a good week at work."

Standing there, I bit down on my bottom lip and frowned as he walked out the door.

"Have a good week at work." Was he planning not to contact me next week? I threw myself down on the bed and stared up at the ceiling. The weekend spent with him was probably the best couple of days I'd ever had in my life. The sex, the food, the fun; it was all like a dream, but I still didn't know anything else about him except that his parents were deceased and relationships were off the table. Going back to that conversation, I played it over and over in my head. What could have made him think like that? Why would he think like that? As I was pondering my thoughts and already missing him, there was a knock at the door. Jumping up from the bed, my heart started racing at the thought of seeing him again.

"Mom. Dad." I tried not to sound disappointed.

"Oh good, you're home. We were in the area and thought we'd drop by for a visit." My mom smiled as she kissed my cheek.

"Your mother wants the scoop on your romp in Vegas with that rich guy," my dad spoke as he went into my refrigerator and pulled out a beer.

"Shush up, Larry. So," my mom placed her hand on my arm, "How did it go?"

"It was wonderful." I smiled brightly and then went into the kitchen to make some tea.

"Are the two of you dating?" she asked.

"Here's the thing." I turned and looked at her. "We had a slight conversation and he threw it out there that he doesn't latch on to anyone and relationships are off the table."

"Oh. That's strange. Did he say why?"

"Nope. He changed the subject. When I asked about his parents, he told me that they died years ago and he didn't want to talk about it."

"Poor man. It sounds like he has a tortured soul. Maybe he just needs some guidance." She smiled.

After pouring the hot water into the cups, I took them over with the teabags to the table.

"I don't know, Mom. On one hand, he has a kind and gentle soul, and on the other, I sense a darkness about him."

"You don't think he's dangerous, do you?"

"No. Of course not. I get the feeling something happened in his past that he's hiding. I don't know. He's just very closed off personally."

She reached her hand over and placed it on top of mine.

"Well, maybe you're just the girl he needs to bring light into his life. Maybe he needs a spiritual cleansing. Why don't you have him come over to our apartment and I can help him with that?"

"Somehow, I don't think he'd go for that. He doesn't believe in that stuff. He gambled last night."

She frowned. "Oh. We're in a Venus retrograde. That wasn't a good idea."

"I warned him, but he didn't listen and lost thousands."

After a long conversation and we finished our tea, she got up from her chair. "Larry, we need to get going."

"Coming," my dad said as he got up from the couch. "It's nice to have you back home, pumpkin." He kissed my cheek.

I walked them to the door and then went into the bathroom to take a nice long, relaxing bath.

****

Sebastian

"How did it go?" Eli asked on our drive to the penthouse.

"It went well. We had a great time. She asked about my parents again."

"What did you tell her?"

"I told her they've been dead for years and I didn't want to talk about it."

"I hate to break the news to you, Sebastian, but if you're going to continue to see Chloe, you're going to have to tell her about your childhood."

"Who says I'm going to continue to see her? I took her to Vegas on a whim. It meant nothing."

He looked at me through the rearview mirror.

"Okay, but I think—"

"Drop it, Eli. I don't want to talk about Chloe Kane anymore."

Stepping inside the penthouse, I set my bag down, and Karina, my maid, immediately picked it up.

"Welcome home, Mr. Bennett."

"Thank you. Did you pick up my dry cleaning?"

"Yes, sir. Your suits are hanging in your closet."

"Good. I have an important meeting tomorrow. Also, make sure that you unpack my bag."

"Yes, sir."

Walking over to the bar, I poured myself a drink and took it out on the patio. I couldn't shake the thoughts that were swimming around in my head about Chloe. This weekend was good, really good, and I enjoyed spending time with her. Feeling her naked body pressed against mine while we slept did wonders for me. I hadn't slept that good in years, actually, not since London. I pulled my ringing phone from my pocket and noticed it was the Palazzo Hotel calling.

"Hello," I answered.

"Mr. Bennett, this is Cassandra at the Palazzo Hotel. I just wanted to inform you that your hotel bill was already paid, so we won't be charging the credit card you have on file."

"What do you mean it's already been paid? By whom?"

"The woman that was staying in the room with you. She left cash in an envelope this morning at the front desk with a note stating that the room was to be paid for using that."

Shaking my head, I sighed. "Okay. Thank you for calling and letting me know."

That woman. I couldn't believe she did that. I quickly typed out a text message but deleted it. I wanted her to hear the anger in my voice.

"Hello," she answered.

"Chloe, it's Sebastian. What the hell were you thinking?" I asked in a stern voice.

"Hi, Sebastian. What are you talking about?"

"I just received a call from the hotel we stayed at in Vegas. They kindly informed me that you paid the hotel bill with the cash you won."

"Oh. Yeah. It was their money anyway, so why not give it back? Why are you so mad about it?"

I could feel the heat rising inside my veins.

"Because that was your money!" I shouted. "I told you to go and buy something nice with it and you chose to pay the goddamn hotel bill instead."

"First of all, you need to calm down. Second of all, if you claim it was my money, then I can choose to spend it however I want to and I chose to pay the hotel bill."

I clenched my fist and slowly closed my eyes for a moment to keep from really losing my cool with her.

"I am more than capable of paying the hotel bill!" I shouted.

"Breathe, Sebastian."

"What?"

"Take in a long deep breath. Do you meditate?"

"What? Meditate? No, I don't meditate!"

"Well, you should. Now I have to go. I'm in the middle of taking a relaxing bath and you so rudely interrupted me with this hotel nonsense."

I heard a click and pulled my phone from my ear. She hung up on me. Damn her.

"It seems Miss Kane has you all worked up." Eli smiled as he walked out on the patio.

"Can you believe that she paid the hotel bill with the money she won in Vegas?" I threw back my drink.

"That was nice of her."

"Nice of her? It was stupid. I told her to go buy something nice for herself. Then she said it was the hotel's money anyway, so why not give it back. What kind of fucking reasoning is that?"

"The reasoning of a woman who doesn't believe in material things."

Rolling my eyes, I went back inside and poured another bourbon.

"Yeah, well, whether she believes in them or not, she shouldn't have done that. And another thing, do you know she won all that money because the sun was in Leo and I lost thousands last night because supposedly we're in a Venus retrograde?"

"Huh. She's into astrology. Interesting." He smirked.

I shook my finger at him. "Do you know what she just asked me?"

"What?"

"She asked me if I meditate. She's way out there, Eli. Her mother is a spiritual advisor and her dad is a musician on the streets of the New York."

He just stood there with a grin on his face. "Yeah. She's way out there all right. Too good for you, may I add."

"What the hell is that supposed to mean?"

"Nothing. I'll see you tomorrow unless you need me to drive you somewhere tonight."

"No." I waved my hand. "I'm in for the night. I have work to do."

He walked away and I finished off my drink.

"Mr. Bennett," Karina spoke. "Dinner will be ready shortly."

"Thank you, Karina."

I went to my room and changed out of my clothes and into something a little more comfortable. Taking a seat at the dining table, I began to eat my dinner. For the first time in two and a half days, I was alone. Which was good, right? She annoyed me at times. Got under my skin and made me question why I even brought her to Vegas. I smiled at the thought of her. Shaking my head, I made all thoughts disappear. I needed to focus on other things, like business. I didn't become what I was today by slacking on my work. The only way to get her completely off my mind was to avoid all contact with her for a while. I had a deal that was ready to go through and it was an important one. One that would make me millions.

Chapter 19

Chloe

"You probably emasculated him," Sienna said as she bit into her turkey avocado wrap.

"No. Sebastian would never feel like that."

"Really? He's a hot and sexy gazillionaire. Do you actually think some of the women he's been with have ever paid his hotel bill? It's what he does, Chloe. He's rich, powerful, and from what I can tell, a control freak. You, my loving spirited friend, who tries to make everyone happy by doing the right thing, emasculated him."

"Ugh." I took a sip of my water.

After finishing our lunch, Sienna left the gallery and headed back to work. I couldn't help but wonder if what she said was true. Oh well, I had too much work to do to get ready for Caden's exhibition to worry about Sebastian feeling emasculated.

As I was standing in front of the wall with a swatch of paint samples in my hand, I heard Connor and Ellery walk up the stairs. Turning around, Ellery gave me a hug.

"I heard you were in Vegas with Sebastian. How did it go?"

"It went great. We had a good time and a lot of fun."

She stared at me with a smirk on her face. A smirk that told me she wanted all the juicy details.

"Have you decided on a color?" Connor asked.

"Almost. It's between these two." I held the swatches up against the wall.

"Both are great choices." He smiled. "Have you contacted the painter?"

"Yes, and he said just to let him know when I pick a color and he'll be right over. He said it should only take a day to get it done."

"Good. So, things went well with Sebastian?" Connor asked in a weird way.

"Yes." I narrowed my eye at him. "Did you think they wouldn't?"

"Oh. No. Not at all. I was just asking."

"What Connor means is that Sebastian has quite a reputation for being a ladies' man and—"

I put my hand up.

"I know all about his reputation. It's sweet that the two of you worry about me, but you don't have to. I can take care of myself where Sebastian Bennett is concerned."

Ellery scrunched up her nose. "I know you can," she spoke as she placed her hands on my shoulders.

"I do have a question for you, Connor."

"What is it?"

"Pretend you and Ellery weren't married and you just started seeing each other and you took her on a trip with you. Would you have a problem if she paid the hotel bill?"

"I would never let her, so it wouldn't be a problem."

"Let's say she threw some cash in an envelope and sneaked it down to the front desk without you knowing."

His eyebrow arched. "Well, if that was the case, I would have a problem with it. I invited her to go with me, so it would be my responsibility to pay the bill. Why? Did you pay the hotel bill?" He smirked.

"Sebastian gave me some money before he left for his meeting in case I wanted to go down to the casino. I tried to refuse it, but he was very adamant that I took it. So I played a little blackjack and won a lot of money. After arguing when I tried to give him all the money since I won it with what he gave me, he took back the amount he gave and told me to keep the rest and buy something nice with it."

"How sweet." Ellery smiled.

Connor looked over at her with a frown. "I do that all the time."

She patted his arm.

"I didn't feel right keeping it, and Sebastian wouldn't take it back, so I paid the hotel bill. After all, it was the casino's money, so I was just giving it back to them. The hotel ended up calling Sebastian and telling him about it and he was a bit angry."

Connor scratched his head. "You gave the money back to the hotel?"

"Technically, since it was their money I won."

"Aw, that was so nice of you to do that, sweetie." Ellery smiled.

"It wasn't my money to keep anyway, but Sebastian can't understand that."

"I don't blame him. I can't understand it either," Connor spoke.

"Of course you don't, Connor. You're money hungry." Ellery frowned. "You did a great thing, Chloe, and if Sebastian is angry over it, too bad."

"My friend Sienna said that he probably feels emasculated."

"I'm sure he does," Connor spoke.

"Well, he did lose a crap load of money the night before. I warned him not to gamble, since we were in the beginning of a Venus retrograde."

"Huh?" Connor cocked his head.

Ellery stood there and shook her head at him. "Come on, Connor, you have a meeting to get to and I have some shopping to do with Peyton. We'll talk later and see you tonight at dinner. Per Se at seven thirty."

"Looking forward to it." I smiled.

I was meeting Connor and Ellery for dinner. It wasn't just any ordinary dinner. It was a celebratory dinner for the success of opening night at the gallery. Both had felt bad that they didn't get a chance to do it sooner, but as far as I was concerned, they didn't need to do it at all. After they left, I examined the swatches one last time and finally picked a color.

****

Sebastian

I hadn't contacted Chloe all week after our little discussion about the hotel bill. I was still pissed off that she would do that and not even tell me. As I was sitting at my desk, my phone rang. It was Serena.

"Hello, Serena."

"Your voice is music to my ears, Sebastian. I haven't heard from you in a while. How about dinner tonight?"

Leaning back in my chair, I placed my hand on my forehead.

"Sure. Why not? Where do you want to meet?"

"How about Per Se at seven o'clock?"

"Very good. I'll see you at seven."

Serena was a woman whom I saw on occasion. She was the daughter of J.P Morgan of JP Morgan Chase. She was classy, elegant, and sophisticated. She was exactly what I needed right now.

"I just have to change my clothes," I spoke to Eli as we entered the penthouse.

"Are we picking Miss Kane up?" he asked.

I stopped and looked at him. "I'm not seeing Chloe tonight. I'm having dinner with Serena."

"I see." He frowned.

After changing and dabbing on some more Armani cologne, Eli and I headed to the limo.

"Have you spoken to Chloe since your little irate phone call to her?"

"No. Why would I?"

"You did take her on a trip, Sebastian."

"So what. Like I said before, it didn't mean anything. You know me, Eli. I don't attach myself to anyone."

"I know, but I thought this time—"

"You thought wrong. So please, keep your opinions to yourself."

"I've known you for many years, Sebastian, and this woman has affected you like no other woman has in your lifetime."

"No she hasn't, so don't go assuming things you know nothing about."

He rolled his eyes and drove me to Per Se.

Chapter 20

Chloe

Connor, Ellery, and I arrived at the restaurant at the same time. After promptly being seated, Connor ordered a bottle of wine. Once the glasses were filled, Connor held his up.

"To a very successful opening night and to the woman who made it happen." He smiled.

"I second that." Ellery held up her glass.

"Thank you. But this wasn't necessary. You already know that I appreciate everything you've done for me."

"It was necessary and we appreciate everything you've done for us and the gallery." Ellery smiled.

After looking over our menus, we placed our dinner order and I looked around the restaurant.

"This place is so—" I stopped midsentence and stared across the room.

"What's wrong?" Connor asked.

"Umm." My eyes wouldn't leave the table where Sebastian and a woman were sitting.

Connor and Ellery both turned around and then turned back and looked at me.

"Damn him," Connor spewed.

"No. No. It's fine. Trust me." I gave a fake smile. "I was just a little surprised. I'm okay."

"We can leave. Right, Connor?" Ellery asked.

"Of course."

"No. We're staying and enjoying a wonderful dinner."

"Are you sure? Do you want me to claw his eyes out?" Ellery pouted.

"Oh, God, Ellery. Please don't make a scene." Connor shook his head.

"Thanks for the offer, Ellery, but I'm fine. It's not like we were a couple or anything. He told me that relationships were off the table. So he can see anybody he wants."

Hurt coursed through my body and when it reached my heart, it hurt pretty bad. I wanted to cry, but I wouldn't. I wouldn't shed a tear for a man who could do what he did.

"If you'll excuse me, I need to use the restroom," Connor spoke as he got up from the table.

Ellery held up her hand and signaled our waiter. "Four shots of Jack Daniels, please."

"Coming right up, Mrs. Black."

"When you're hurting, Jack is the one man you can count on that will always be there for you. He'll listen and then he'll make you feel oh so good." She smiled.

I couldn't help but laugh. When I looked across the room, I saw Connor stop at Sebastian's table before returning to ours.

"Shit." I looked down. "Connor stopped at their table."

"Of course he did, because he knew I would eventually make it over there."

Connor came back to the table, and when I looked across the room, Sebastian was staring at me. Like an idiot, I gave him a small smile and wave.

"Did you just smile and wave at him?" Ellery whispered as she leaned across the table.

"Yes."

"Good job." She held up her hand for a high five.

"What did you say to him?" I asked.

"Nothing. I just told him it was nice to see him and that you were here with us celebrating the success of opening night. You should have seen the look on his face when he looked over and saw you sitting here."

"Yeah, because he got caught. The sorry son of a bitch," Ellery spoke.

"He didn't get caught at anything. We aren't dating. So let's enjoy our dinner and talk about something else."

The waiter brought our shots of whiskey and set them in the middle of the table.

"Are those what I think they are?" Connor asked Ellery.

"Yes."

"Elle, this isn't the kind of restaurant where you do shots."

"Connor, sweetheart. As long as a place has a bar and serves alcohol, shots can be done anywhere."

He sighed and shifted in his chair. I laughed. After doing the first shot, I set the glass down and closed my eyes. The burn felt so good. Picking up the second glass, I brought it to my lips just as Sebastian approached our table.

"Hello, Chloe. Ellery." He nodded.

"Hello, Sebastian." I smiled and gulped at the same time. I needed to hold it together even though my heart was racing and my legs were shaking under the table.

"I hope you're enjoying your dinner."

"We are, Sebastian. How was Vegas?" Ellery grinned.

I looked over at Connor and he placed his hand over his face.

"Vegas was good." Sebastian looked at me.

"Good. Good to hear. Connor and I love Vegas. Where did you and Chloe stay? You know, in Vegas, together for an entire weekend?"

"The Palazzo Hotel."

"Nice. We usually stay at the Bellagio."

"Well, I'll let you get back to your dinner. It was nice seeing the three of you."

He gave me a small smile as he walked away. His lips might have been smiling, but his eyes told a different story.

"Why did you bring up Vegas?" Connor asked as he glared at Ellery.

"Why not? He's wrong and he knows it. Someone had to call him out on his bullshit."

"But—"

"No buts, Connor."

I simply sat there across from this adorable couple and smiled. After we finished eating, we said our goodbyes.

"Call me if you want to talk." Ellery hugged me.

"I'm fine, Ellery. But I promise I will."

"I'll be in touch, Chloe," Connor spoke as he hugged me. "Have a good night. I'm sorry about what happened."

"Don't be. Maybe it's the universe sending me a sign." I smiled.

****

Sebastian

Fuck. Fuck. Fuck. I ran my hands through my hair as Serena and I exited the restaurant.

"Let's go back to my place," Serena whispered in my ear.

Yeah. That was what I needed. I needed to fuck her and release this tension that had been brewing inside me the last few days.

"Let's go." I hooked my arm around her and we walked to the limo.

As I slid in next to her, Eli shot me a look. I turned and looked out the passenger window to avoid any further eye contact with him. He didn't know shit. When we stepped inside Serena's apartment, she asked me to unzip her dress. Taking off my suit coat, my fingers deftly grasped her zipper and slowly pulled it down. My lips traveled to her shoulder as I slipped off her dress and let it fall to the ground. She turned to face me and our lips locked tightly together. She moaned. My hands cupped her bare breasts, kneading them and tugging at her hardened nipples.

"God, I've missed this, Sebastian," she moaned as my lips traveled to her neck.

Thoughts of Chloe went off in my head like a slide show. Me fucking her. Her smile. Her laugh. Her incredibly sexy body and her beautiful green eyes. Eyes that could light up a dark room. Eyes that smiled at me every time I looked into them. Pulling away, I put my hand up.

"I'm sorry, Serena. I can't."

"What do you mean you can't? Come on, baby." She smiled as her lips brushed against mine.

"I can't." I pulled away and paced around the room.

"What the fuck is the matter with you?" she shouted rather loudly.

"I have to go."

Grabbing my jacket, I left her apartment and climbed into the limo.

"That sure as hell didn't take very long," Eli spoke.

"That's because nothing happened. Just drive."

When I arrived home, I poured myself a drink and took it out on the patio. What the hell was happening to me? I needed to call her and make sure she was okay. Her phone rang and then went straight to voicemail. She ignored my call. Great. I sent her a text message.

"Chloe, I think we need to talk about tonight."

I waited for a response and nothing. Slamming my glass down on the table, I flew out the door and hailed a cab to her apartment. As I was walking up the steps, a couple came walking out. I ran and held the door open for them and then headed up the stairs to Chloe's apartment. I softly knocked and waited. No answer. I knocked again. No answer. Pulling out my phone, I sent her a text message.

"Damn it, Chloe! Answer the fucking door!"

As I hit the send button, I heard her voice down the hallway.

"Sebastian? What are you doing here?" She cocked her head while holding a large brown bag in her hands.

"Doesn't matter. What matters is I don't appreciate my calls or text messages being ignored," I spoke in an abrupt tone.

"Huh? I didn't get any calls or text messages from you." She handed me the large paper bag as she slid her key in the lock.

"Don't lie to me, Chloe." I followed her inside.

She pulled her phone from her purse. "It's dead. That's why I didn't get anything from you. See for yourself." She held up her phone.

She took it into the kitchen and plugged the charger into it. Then, she turned and narrowed her eyes at me.

"Just ignore that last text," I said. "Why are you going to Whole Foods so late? Do you know how dangerous that is?"

She started removing the groceries from the bag and set them on the counter.

"I needed a few things and on my way home, I stopped and talked to Willie. We had a nice conversation and then I gave him some apples. Actually, I gave him all the apples I bought, so I guess I'll have to go back tomorrow and get some more."

"Who the hell is Willie?" I stood there in confusion at the fact that she gave him apples.

"The nice homeless man that resides on the next block. During the day, he camps out in front of Barnes and Nobles, and at night, he moves to the alley. But he was still at Barnes and Noble when I walked by."

"May I ask why you talk to him?"

"Why wouldn't I talk to him? He's an interesting person. He served in the military for thirty years and fought in two wars and received the Medal of Honor."

"Then why is he homeless?"

"When his kids grew up, his wife left him. He started drinking heavily, lost his job, couldn't afford his house, so the bank took it and now he's on the street. It's sad that he's been living like that for five years."

"It's his own fault. He could do something, but he chooses not to. So he has no one to blame but himself."

"Wow, Sebastian, that's really cold-hearted."

"It's the truth, Chloe. You know it, and the fact that you even talk to him."

She sighed. "He's a human being just like you and me. Is there a reason you came over, because I'm really tired and would like to go to bed?"

"I think we need to talk about tonight."

"What about it?"

"I wanted to explain about Serena."

"I don't care about her. You obviously had your reasons for going to dinner with her. It's none of my business." She placed her hands on the counter.

"It was just dinner. If there were more, I wouldn't be standing here in your apartment."

"Like I said, it's none of my business."

Walking over to her, I placed my hand on her cheek.

"Good night, Sebastian," she spoke as she stared into my eyes.

"Do you really want me to leave, Chloe?"

"Yes." She didn't hesitate to answer.

Removing my hand from her cheek, I lightly kissed her forehead.

"I'll be in touch," I spoke as I began to walk away.

"Please don't," she said in a low voice.

With my back turned to her, I stopped and looked down. Taking in a deep breath, I walked out of her apartment and hailed a cab back home. The pain I had buried so long ago was back. I felt it in my chest. I felt it when I looked at her. She claimed she didn't care, but she did. Her eyes, which were always full of light, were now filled with sadness.

Chapter 21

Chloe

Placing the last piece of art on the wall, I stood back and studied the display we all helped organize.

"It's truly a beautiful sight." Gregory sighed.

"It sure is."

"Everyone that we sent invites to has responded that they will be attending. This is going to be huge." He smiled.

"What about Mr. Bennett?" I asked as I looked at Gregory.

"He responded with a no."

"That's good. It's probably for the best. I'm going to finish up some work and take the rest of the day off. I think I'll go see my dad."

When I walked into my office, my phone rang. It was Sienna.

"Hey." I hit the answer button and set my phone on the metal stand on my desk.

"So I have a bit of a problem."

"What's wrong?"

She rested her cheek in her hand. "I hate that Sam went back to England."

"Aw, Sienna. I can honestly say I'm shocked."

"I know, right? Me too. I miss the big goofball already and he's only been gone a couple of hours."

"I think someone is in love." I smiled.

"Maybe. Who knows. He cried at the airport."

"He did?"

"Yeah." I could see her eyes start to fill with tears.

"He told me that he loved me and if I loved him, he'd stay."

"I'm assuming you didn't tell him."

"I told him that I'd have to get back to him on that."

"OMG! Sienna."

"He freaked me out. I panicked. Listen, I have to go. My pain in the ass client is standing at the door looking at me."

"Okay. Call me later or come over. We can do a girls' night and sit on the couch with our gallon of ice cream and watch depressing movies."

"Sounds like a plan."

Shaking my head, I cleaned up my desk, grabbed my purse, and headed out the door to see my dad. As I approached East 42nd Street, I saw him sitting on the ground Indian style with his guitar in his hand.

"Hey, Dad." I smiled as I sat down next to him.

"Hey, pumpkin. You're going to get your fancy pants all dirty."

"They can be washed. How's business?" I asked, looking over at his guitar case, which was filled with green.

"It's a good day. You know why?"

"Why?"

"Because it's a beautiful May day and everyone is in a good mood. Here." He handed me his guitar. "Drum up some more business for your old man."

With a grin, I took the guitar from him. This was something we did on occasion. I began playing and singing *Tomorrow Is a Long Time* by Nickel Creek. Before long, people stopped to listen as they threw dollar bills into the guitar case. My heart started racing as I was singing and looked up to see Sebastian standing amongst the crowd of people staring at me. When I finished the song, He walked over with his hands tucked into his pockets.

"Why, hello there, Sebastian." My dad smiled.

"Hello, Larry. Chloe." He nodded.

Handing my dad back his guitar, I gave him a kiss on his cheek.

"I'll talk to you later, Dad."

"Yeah. Okay. Enjoy the rest of your day, pumpkin."

I began to walk away and Sebastian walked with me.

"You were really good," he spoke.

"Thanks." I stared straight ahead.

"So how have you been?"

I swallowed hard. "Fine. Busy. You?"

"Okay. I guess. Busy as well."

"Good." I turned the corner.

"Chloe, listen. I want to see you."

"You're seeing me."

He lightly grabbed hold of my arm and forced me to stop walking.

"I want to see you. Let's have dinner together tonight at my place."

As I stood there and stared into his pleading eyes, a part of me wanted to slap him.

"I can't. I'm sorry."

"You can't or you won't?" He cocked his head.

"I can't. Sienna is coming over tonight. Sam went back to England today and she's really sad, so we're going to have a girls' night in."

"I see. How about tomorrow?"

"Sorry. I have an exhibition tomorrow."

"That's right. How about after the exhibition? We can have a late dinner."

"I don't know." I began walking. Why was the thought of possibly having dinner with him going through my head?

"Just dinner. Nothing else. I promise."

"Dinner at your place and you expect me to believe you won't try to have sex?"

"I promise. I'll be on my best behavior. Please, Chloe, just have dinner with me."

His begging was pathetic. I stopped.

"Fine. I'll have dinner with you after the exhibition. Gregory told me that you responded no on the invite."

"Now that you've agreed to have dinner with me, I've changed my mind. I'll be there." The corners of his mouth curved upwards.

"Were you going somewhere before you saw me with my dad?"

"Oh shit. I was meeting Damien. I'll see you tomorrow night at the gallery."

"Okay."

As I walked away, Sebastian called my name.

"Chloe."

"Yeah?" I turned around.

"Have a fun girls' night tonight." He smiled.

"Thanks."

I was nothing but the poster child for being a glutton for punishment.

****

Sebastian

I barely slept a wink all night. Not only was I thinking about Chloe, but also about this big deal I was signing today. This had been in the making for months, and it was one of the biggest deals I'd made in a long time.

Sitting in the conference room alone, I had an unsettling feeling. I didn't know where it came from or why, but something was really bothering me. Ed and John walked in and Damien followed behind.

"Hello, Sebastian. Do you have your signing pen ready?" Ed smiled as he set the contracts in front of me.

"You've made the right decision to become a capital investor in our company," John spoke as he took a seat.

Looking over the contracts, my unsettled feeling didn't diminish. What the fuck was going on? "Gentlemen, excuse me for a moment." Pulling my phone from my pocket, I sent a text message to Chloe.

"Good morning. Are we still in that Venus thing?"

"You mean a Venus retrograde? Yes. For about another four weeks. Why?"

"Just wondering. So now wouldn't be a good time to make a major business investment?"

"No. Not a good time at all."

"Thank you. I'll see you later."

"You're welcome. Do you want to tell me what all this is about?"

"Later."

Walking back into the conference room, I took a seat across from Ed and John.

"I'm sorry, gentlemen, but I'm not signing any contracts at this time."

"WHAT?!" Ed shouted.

"Sebastian," Damien spoke.

"I'll look this over again in about a month. Until then, I won't be investing in your company. I'm sorry. Now if you'll excuse me, I have other work to do."

Getting up from my chair, I buttoned my suit coat and walked out. *Fuck.* I prayed to God that I made the right decision. Damien followed me into my office.

"What the fuck, Sebastian? What the hell are you thinking? We worked months on that deal. Do you know how much money you just cost us?"

Taking a seat at my desk, I arched my brow at him.

"Us? This is my company and I make every damn decision about it. Don't you ever forget that." I pointed at him. "Right now isn't the right time to invest in that company."

"And how do you know that?"

"I'm going with my instincts. You need to trust me on this, Damien. Have I ever steered off course where this company is concerned?"

He sat there shaking his head with a look of anger on his face. Getting up from his seat, he pointed at me before walking out the door.

"You better hope your instincts are right. You've been off ever since that girl walked into your life."

Rolling my eyes, I leaned back in my chair. He was right where Chloe was concerned. I had been off. It seemed like my whole life had been turned upside down ever since that one night in London.

Chapter 22

Chloe

I nervously walked around the gallery, watching, staring, and hearing the whispers of the people who came to the exhibition. Connor and Ellery were standing in front of the sculptures talking to Oliver and Liam Wyatt. There was no reason to be nervous, but I was. I think I was more nervous for Caden. Looking at my watch, I wondered where Sienna was. Suddenly, I felt two arms wrap around my waist from behind.

"Hello, gorgeous."

Turning my head, I gasped when I saw Sam staring at me.

"Oh my God. What are you doing here?"

"When I landed in Boston, I couldn't get on that next plane. I just couldn't do it. I already missed her too much."

"Aw. Where is Sienna?"

"She's in the bathroom. She told me to come up and surprise you."

"Well, I'm glad you did." I placed my hand on his chest.

"SURPRISE!" Sienna smiled as she held out her arms.

Hugging her tightly, I could tell she was happy that Sam was back.

"This is a great surprise, right?" I whispered in her ear.

"Yes. It sure is. I'll fill you in on all the details later. For now, I'm going to check out that sexy artwork over there."

She hooked her arm in Sam's and the two of them walked over to the display.

"I thought he went back to England." I heard Sebastian's voice behind me.

When I turned around, the butterflies awoke in my belly as if they were happy to see him.

"He never made it out of Boston. He came back."

"I see. How are you?" He smiled.

"Nervous, but good."

Placing his hand on my shoulder, he spoke, "Don't be nervous. It looks like everyone is enjoying the exhibition. I will admit that I am curious to see what the artist has done."

"Then follow me." I smiled as I held out my arm to him and led him over to the display. "Well?" I asked.

"It definitely is erotic, that's for sure.

"You like it, though, right?"

"Yes. It's very expressive."

"Exactly!" I smiled.

"He does photography too?" Sebastian asked as he stared at the beautiful naked girl in the stiletto heels with the pouty mouth.

"Yes." I laughed. "Do you like her?" I nudged his shoulder.

"Who me? She's not my type." He winked.

I wanted to ask him what his type was, but I refrained for fear he'd get angry.

"Hello, Sebastian." Ellery smiled.

"Hello, Ellery. You're looking as lovely as ever." He kissed her cheek.

"Thank you. If you don't mind, I'm going to steal Chloe away for a moment."

"I don't mind at all."

When I walked away with Ellery, she led me downstairs.

"Richard Borne is very interested in purchasing almost half the display. He wants a couple paintings, five photographs, and two sculptures."

"What's he going to do with all that?"

"Apparently, he has a," she held her fingers up, "room that they would be perfect in."

"Ah. I bet it's a very special room." I smiled.

"Ew!" she shrieked. "Him and that room. The thought." She laughed. "Go ahead and talk to Mr. Borne and find out exactly which pieces he wants and put sold stickers on them."

"I'm on it. Caden will be very happy."

"So will Connor."

Walking back up the stairs, I went into my office and pulled the sold stickers from my desk and found Mr. Borne. The exhibition was well received and Caden sold almost every piece of artwork. Standing there staring at the wall that was devoid of all but three paintings, I felt a hand softly touch my back.

"The exhibition went well," Sebastian spoke. "I told you that you had nothing to worry about."

"It did. Didn't it? I'm really happy for Caden."

"If you're ready, we can head to my penthouse for dinner."

"I'm more than ready. I'm starving. Just let me grab my purse."

Grabbing my purse from my office, I left the gallery in the hands of Gregory to close up and Sebastian and I headed to his penthouse.

****

"Wow," I spoke in awe as I looked around his forty-five-hundred-square-foot penthouse. The light beige walls and light oak flooring made the space look even bigger.

"So what do you think of my stuffy penthouse?" The corners of his mouth curved upwards.

"Okay. So I was wrong. It's very light and airy. No dark wood floors, no dark trim, but I was right about the beige walls."

"Everyone has beige walls." He chuckled.

"Mr. Bennett, dinner is ready."

"Thank you, Karina."

It was apparent that Sebastian wasn't going to introduce me to the hired help. So I introduced myself.

"Hi." I smiled as I held out my hand. "I'm Chloe."

"Nice to meet you. I'm Karina."

"Nice to meet you too, Karina." I narrowed my eye at Sebastian.

I followed him out onto the patio, where a table, next to an outdoor fireplace sat.

"I thought it would be nice to dine out here. Of course, if you get cold, we can move inside."

"No. This is fine." I smiled.

We took our seats and Sebastian picked up the bottle of wine and poured some into our glasses.

"So, are you going to tell me what that text was about earlier today?"

He sighed as he brought the glass up to his lips.

"I was supposed to sign the contracts to become a capital investor in a company I had been dealing with for the past several months. It was a multi-million-dollar deal and I got to thinking about how much I lost in Vegas."

"Go on." I smiled.

"It's not a big deal, Chloe. I just thought that maybe this deal wasn't supposed to happen right now, so I didn't sign the contracts. Needless to say, they were not happy."

"That's too bad for them. You did the right thing." I winked before sipping my wine.

We talked mostly about the exhibition, my job, Sienna and Sam, and nothing personally about him. So I decided to turn it into a game.

"I want to play a game."

"Oh." His eyebrow arched. "What kind of game?"

"A personal game. It's a great way to get to know each other. I'll start."

I could tell by the expression on his face that he was on the fence about it.

"My favorite color is yellow." I pointed at him.

"Black."

"My favorite food is chicken." I pointed at him.

"Lobster.

"My favorite kind of flower is the gerbera daisy." I pointed at him.

"You don't like roses?" He cocked his head.

"Yes. Answer the question."

"Orchids."

"Really?" I smiled.

"If I had to pick one favorite flower, it would be them."

"I was sixteen when I lost my virginity." I pointed at him.

"Fifteen." He smiled.

"With who?" I cocked my head.

"Doesn't matter."

"I was homeschooled until the age of ten." I pointed at him.

He didn't say anything and got up from his seat. "That was fun, but I think we should go inside now."

"What's wrong?" I asked as I grabbed my glass and followed him inside.

"Nothing. I want to make something very clear to you. My past and childhood are off limits."

"I don't understand." I frowned.

He ran his hand through his hair. "I don't talk about my past to anyone, including you."

"But why?" I asked in a soft voice as I stepped closer to him.

"Because I don't." His voice was authoritative and harsh. "If you can't respect that, then maybe you should leave."

"You can talk to me, Sebastian."

As I went to place my hand on his arm, he backed away.

"No, Chloe, I can't and I won't."

"How am I supposed to get to know you if you won't open up to me?"

"You know enough. Leave it at that. It's not like you need to know anymore."

"You're right." I looked down. "I know enough. You have so much hatred in your heart and I feel sorry for you. But I know somewhere in there you have more good. I've seen it and I've experienced it." I grabbed my purse and as I was about to walk out the door, I turned and looked at him. "Life is lost without love, Sebastian, and I hope someday you find it."

Chapter 23

Sebastian

Standing there, I watched the door close. She was gone and, suddenly, my place felt empty, or was it my life? An empty feeling always resided in me from the time I could remember when I was a small child. Her words replayed over and over in my head. "Life is lost without love." I didn't know what love was. How could I? I'd never received it and I never gave it. I had once again hurt her. Just like I knew I would. I should've stayed away, but when I saw her on the street, playing the guitar, and her sweet voice sang that song, everything that I thought I had pushed away came rushing back. Just like it did the first time I saw her after our one night together.

Two weeks had passed. I didn't contact her and she didn't try to contact me. Anger made itself a comfortable place inside me. I couldn't focus, I couldn't think, and I certainly couldn't have sex. I didn't want to have sex with anyone but her. She somehow left her mark on me, like an imprint on my soul. Sitting at the bar with Eli, we kicked back some drinks. He was the only person in the world who truly knew me and that was because we had been friends since we were ten years old.

"I think it's time we had a talk, Sebastian."

"About what?"

"These past couple of weeks, you've been different. Different than I've ever seen you before."

"How?" I shot him a look.

"You haven't been going into the office as much. You've been sleeping in later than you ever have. You don't listen when people talk to you. It's like you're in another world and you're way more of an asshole now than before. Damien told me that he asked you the other day what was wrong and you nearly castrated him."

I threw back my bourbon. "I'm tired of people asking me what the hell is wrong. Nothing is wrong!"

"Chloe is what's wrong. Man, come on. I know you're thinking she could be the one and it scares the fuck out of you."

Rolling my eyes, I signaled the bartender for another drink.

"I don't believe in 'the one.'"

"Really? Because you've dated countless women over the years and not one of them has ever gotten to you like Chloe has. If you want to see her again, you're going to have to open up to her."

"I don't have to do anything. I make my own rules about my life and you know it." I pointed my finger at him.

"I know, but maybe now it's time to let the fucking rules go. Damnit, Sebastian, you're thirty years old. Are you really going to live the rest of your life like this? Shit, even Maura is worried about you."

"You can tell Maura that I'm fine."

"You say you don't believe in the one, yet you wouldn't sign a multi-million-dollar deal because of some Venus thing, which, by the way, you got from Chloe. All I'm saying is that you need to let go of the past. You beat it. We beat it. The only reason I'm working for your dumb ass is because someone needs to look after you."

"You're working for me because I pay you incredibly well."

"That too." He smiled. "Listen, man, you're happy when she's around. Why can't you, for once in your life, accept some happiness? Don't you think it's about time?"

I glanced over at him for a moment and then looked straight ahead as I finished my drink.

"She's good for you."

"Really? And you know what's good for me? She's different and she lives in another world. Do you know that she talks to a homeless man and buys him food? She knows his damn life story."

"What's wrong with that? She's a friendly person who apparently doesn't judge people. She doesn't seem to be into materialistic things, so you know right there she wasn't seeing you for your money."

"We're from two different worlds, Eli."

"You might want to rethink that because it wasn't that long ago you were pretty much homeless yourself. You've only been in "this" world for the past nine years. Maybe it's you who lives in a different world, not her."

I clenched my jaw. "I'm done talking about her. It could never work and I would ultimately destroy her. She'd want things from me I could never give. Sure, I could give her all the riches of the world, but deep down, I could never give her what she truly needs or wants."

Eli sighed as he finished his drink. "Whatever, my friend. You really need to go talk to someone or you really need to get your head out of your ass. You've never tried giving anything of yourself to anyone, so you don't know shit. Let's go. I'm taking you home."

****

Chloe

It had been three weeks since I'd heard from Sebastian. I tried my hardest not to think about him, but it was impossible. My feelings for him, even though he was a total douchebag, were strong, and I missed him. I threw myself into my work, attended my mother's yoga classes at night, and meditated just about every day. I did anything and everything just to keep my mind off of him.

Walking down the street on my way to the grocery store, I stopped when I saw Willie leaning up against the brick of Barnes and Noble.

"Hey, Willie." I smiled.

"Chloe. Haven't seen you in a while. Where you been?"

"Around. How are you?"

"Same." He grinned. He patted the empty space next to him. "Sit down."

Sitting on the cement, Indian style, I began to play with a small stone that was in front of me.

"What's wrong? You seem sad. You're never sad."

"Tomorrow's my birthday and I was hoping to celebrate it with someone, but unfortunately, we aren't seeing each other anymore. Not that we were really seeing each other, I guess. We were having a lot of sex."

"So then what's the problem? If you were having a lot of sex, it had to be good."

I smiled. "It was, but he won't tell me anything about his past. No matter how hard I try to get him to open up to me, he won't. He wants to know everything about me, yet he refuses to tell me anything about himself."

"Where did you meet this guy?"

"Now there's a story." I grinned. "We met at a hotel bar in London and we had sex. He was my sex with a stranger in a foreign country. We didn't even know each other's names. I was planning on sneaking out in the morning before he woke up, but he beat me to it. When I moved back to New York, we saw each other again. I didn't know he lived here."

"Wow. That's some crazy shit. What are the odds?"

"I know, right?" I held the stone tightly in my hand. "We hooked up again and again and I thought maybe we had something. I guess I was wrong. He told me to accept the fact that he was never going to tell me anything about him, and if I didn't, I could leave. So I did and I haven't spoken to him since."

"Wow. He just let you leave and never tried to contact you?"

"Yep. That's why I'm a little sad right now. But I'll be okay."

"If you want my advice, darling, it's his loss, not yours. You deserve better than that."

"Thanks, Willie." I stood up. "I'm heading over to the store. Any requests?"

"No. You've done enough for me already."

"Nah, don't be silly. I'll pick you up something good." I smiled. "I'll see you later."

Chapter 24

Sebastian

As I was walking down the street, doing some thinking, I happened to glance across and saw Chloe talking to that homeless man. Not only was she talking, but she was pulling things out of the bag she was carrying and giving them to him. I stood there and watched her. Seeing her made me smile, something I hadn't done since the last time I saw her. I waited until she walked away and was out of sight before heading across the street. As I approached the homeless man, he looked up at me.

"Hey, I saw that girl that was just here giving you some things. That was very nice of her."

"Her name is Chloe and she's a wonderful girl. She has a heart of gold, that one. One of the kindest people I have ever met in my life."

Reaching into my pocket, I pulled out a twenty-dollar bill.

"Here. I'm sure you could use this."

He looked at me for a moment and then waved his hand at me.

"Thanks, man. I appreciate it, but I'm okay."

I reached into my pocket and pulled out another twenty.

"Take it. Believe me when I say I don't need it. It would make me feel better if you took it and bought yourself some food or something."

"You're a kind man. Thank you. What's your name?"

"Sebastian." I smiled.

"Nice to meet you, Sebastian. I'm Willie. You married?"

I cocked my head and spoke, "No. I'm not married."

"You would like Chloe. She's not married either. Poor girl is suffering from a broken heart. Maybe you'd like to meet her one day."

"Yeah. Maybe. Have a nice day, Willie."

"You too, Sebastian. Thanks again."

I gave him a small smile and walked away. It hurt me to know that I broke Chloe's heart, but deep down inside, I already knew I had. *Fuck.* I ran my hand through my hair as I walked down the street and climbed into the limo that was waiting at the corner.

"Did I just see you give that homeless man money?" Eli asked.

"Yeah. That's Willie. The man Chloe always talks to."

Eli turned his head and smiled at me but didn't say a word as he pulled out into traffic and took me home.

****

Chloe

Opening my eyes to the bright sun that was shining through the slits of my blinds, I rolled over and thought of Sebastian. Had we been seeing each other, I would have had morning birthday sex. Instead, I was lying here alone on my birthday, feeling like shit because I missed him so much. As I was feeling sorry for myself, my phone rang. When I picked it up from the nightstand, Sienna and Sam appeared on the screen. Did I mention that he quit his job and wanted to permanently move to New York so he could be close to Sienna? I didn't know what he'd do if Sienna decided one day she was done playing with him and tossed him out.

"Happy birthday to you. Happy birthday to you. Happy birthday, dear Chloe. Happy birthday to you!" they both sang.

"Thank you. What a lovely duet." I smiled.

"How does it feel to be twenty-five?" Sienna asked.

"Great. I feel like a certified adult now. I'm officially a quarter of a century year old." I smiled.

They both laughed and Sam blew me a kiss.

After ending our call, I made some coffee and hopped in the shower. The big birthday plans for today included a nice dinner with my mom, dad, Sienna, and Sam, and then afterwards, the three of us were heading to a club where Sienna had planned a big birthday party for me with all of our friends.

As I was sitting at the table sipping my coffee, the buzzer rang. Getting up to answer it, I asked who it was.

"I have a flower delivery for a Miss Chloe Kane," a man with a deep voice spoke.

"I'll buzz you up."

Opening the door, I saw a man with a huge bouquet of flowers coming up the steps.

"Oh my gosh. What beautiful flowers," I spoke as he approached the door.

"Happy birthday, baby."

When the man lowered the bouquet, I nearly squealed when I saw it was Corey.

"OH MY GOD! What are you doing here?" I placed my hands over my mouth.

"Just thought I'd drop by and wish you a happy birthday."

"All the way from California?"

"Yeah. All the way from California." He smiled.

I took the flowers from him and wrapped my arm around his neck.

"I've missed you." I hugged him tightly.

"I've missed you too. Cali isn't the same without you."

"Come on in."

Taking the flowers to the kitchen, I filled a vase with water.

"These are so beautiful. Thank you."

"You're welcome."

"I can't believe you're here." I kissed his lips.

"I'd been planning it for a while. Sienna knew, but I threatened to let secrets spill to that Sam guy she's seeing if she told you."

I laughed. "So how long are you here for?"

"My flight leaves tomorrow afternoon. I have to get back to work. I thought it was time to see you, and what better day than your birthday?"

Corey and I talked on the phone at least twice a week, so he knew all about Sebastian.

"Still no word from that rich asshole?" he asked.

"No." I lowered my head.

"You deserve better than him, Chloe." He placed his thumb on my chin and slightly lifted it so I was looking up at him.

"He can be a wonderful man. If only he'd open up about his past."

"There's a reason he isn't and you need to take that as a universal sign to drop him and run."

I poured him a cup of coffee and we snuggled on the couch, catching up on everything that had been going on in both our lives.

****

Sebastian

I couldn't help myself. I needed to see her. Maybe I was ready to tell her that I cared for her and tell her about my past. This gnawing feeling inside me wouldn't stop until I saw her. Three weeks without her was long enough. I had to make her understand how much I liked her and I needed her to believe that she wasn't just another girl. She was a girl who I wanted to be with all the time. Not talking to her or seeing her left me empty inside. I knew that now and I came to accept the fact that I had to tell her everything about me. She was worth it and I couldn't fight my feelings and desire for her any longer.

I had Eli park around the corner and down the street. Climbing out of the limo and turning the corner, I stopped when I saw her and some guy coming out of her building. She was wearing a short pale pink dress with rhinestone spaghetti straps and matching stiletto heels. She was all dressed up and on the arm of another man. Anger, rage, and jealousy grew inside me as they climbed into the cab that was waiting at the curb. Getting back into the limo, I instructed Eli to follow them.

Waiting in the limo until they were inside Space Ibzia's, I started to climb out when Eli stopped me.

"Sebastian, don't. Leave her alone. Obviously, she's out to have fun tonight. You can talk to her tomorrow."

"NO! I want to know who the fuck that guy is she's with. She's mine, Eli, and I'm going to make sure she knows it."

"Good luck with that. She's not yours. Just because you fucked her, doesn't make her your property. If that was the case, you'd own half of New York City, other states, and countries."

I rolled my eyes. "She's different and she belongs to me."

"You mean she belongs with you."

"Yeah. Whatever. Maybe I won't say anything to her tonight. I just want to see what she's doing. That's all."

"Then I'm coming with you."

I stared at him for a moment before agreeing. He parked the limo down the street and I slipped the bouncer a hundred-dollar bill to let us in.

"No need, Mr. Bennett. I know who you are. You two can go on in."

Giving him a small smile, I placed the bill in his shirt pocket.

Chapter 25

Sebastian

The club was filled with wall-to-wall people. When I paid off two patrons at the bar for their seats, they kindly moved so Eli and I could sit down.

"Two bourbons. Make them doubles," I yelled to the bartender.

Looking around, I didn't see Chloe and that guy anywhere. But who the hell could find anyone in this place.

"Keep an eye out for them," I spoke to Eli.

It had been a little over an hour and still no sign of them. Suddenly, Eli, grabbed my arm and told me that we needed to leave. Glaring at him, I couldn't help but notice his eyes staring at the dance floor. When I looked to where he was looking, I saw Chloe and that asshole dancing together. Her arms were in the air as she moved her hips back and forth. He was behind her, grinding up against her like some pig. The two of them moved around, back and forth with his hands planted on her hips. The rage that was already inside me intensified as I walked up behind them, grabbed the guy's arm, and threw a punch at him, sending him into the crowd of people that surrounded them and to the ground.

"Sebastian!" Chloe screamed.

I wasn't finished because I wanted to make sure this guy never laid his hands on her again. Grabbing his shirt, I punched him again until Eli grabbed my arm and pulled me away.

****

Chloe

I couldn't believe what I was seeing. As I screamed Sebastian's name, he looked at me with rage in his eyes.

"What are you doing?"

"He had no right touching you like that!" he shouted.

Suddenly, Sienna and Sam appeared and Sam got down on the ground to help Corey while Sienna stepped in front of me.

"What the fuck do you think you're doing, Sebastian?"

"Get out of the way, Sienna."

"Or what? Are you going to punch me too?"

"Stop it! Both of you!" I screamed as I stepped away from Sienna.

I shook my head at Sebastian and then bent down to look at Corey. His eye was already swollen and there was blood pouring from his nose and mouth.

"You want him, Chloe? Did you fuck him?" Sebastian screamed as Eli held him back.

Standing up, I stood in front of him. My blood boiling with hatred as I could feel the vein in my temple pulsating with rage.

Placing my hands on his chest, I pushed him as hard as I could. He stumbled.

"He's my ex from California, asshole. He flew in to celebrate my birthday."

His eyes locked with mine and, suddenly, they filled with sadness.

"I'm—"

"Save it, Sebastian. You just can't go around punching people. I never want to see you again." I turned and pushed my way through the crowd of people who were standing there watching the scene.

I needed air. Taking off my shoes and stepping out the door onto the street of New York City, I could barely catch my breath. My body was shaking and I felt disoriented. I fell to my knees on a patch of grass near the club and began crying. Suddenly, I felt a hand on my shoulder.

"Chloe, I'm so sorry. Please forgive me."

Jerking away, I looked up at Sebastian with mascara-stained eyes.

"Don't you touch me!" I shouted as I got up and stumbled back. "Don't touch me," I whispered as I pointed my finger at him. "What part of 'I never want to see you again' did you not understand?"

"I apologized to Corey. He's going to be fine. I just—"

"You're a monster and you are to stay the hell away from me!" I walked away and back inside the club.

"There you are!" Sienna pulled me into a hug. "Are you okay?"

"Not really. Where's Corey?"

"Over here." Sienna led me to a small table where Corey and Sam were seated.

"I'm so sorry this happened." I cried as I wrapped my arms around his neck.

"Don't cry, Chloe. He apologized."

"I don't care. He never should have hit you."

"Listen, I'm fine. It's not the first time I've had a bruised eye and a fat lip." He smiled. "Come on; let's get out of here and go back to your place for cake. We still have more celebrating to do."

****

"Are you sure you feel okay?" I pouted as I gently traced my finger around the bruise on Corey's eye.

"I'm fine. Stop worrying about me. Thanks for letting me crash at your place." He smiled.

"You're welcome to crash at my place any time you come to visit."

"Take care, Chloe, and I'll call you when I land."

"You better." I winked.

"Love you." He kissed my forehead.

"Love you back."

As the cab pulled up to my building, my heart started to race when I saw Sebastian's limo parked at the curb. I swore to God, if he even attempted to talk to me, I would march right down to the police station and file a restraining order against him. After paying the cab driver, I saw Eli step out of the limo. I sat there for a moment while he walked over and opened the door for me.

"Good afternoon, Chloe."

"Eli." I nodded as I climbed out. "He better not be in there." I pointed to the limo.

"He's not. It's just me. In fact, if he knew I was here talking to you, he'd probably fire me."

"What can I do for you, Eli?" I asked as we walked to the door.

"I was hoping to speak with you for a moment about Sebastian."

"I don't want to talk about him."

Sliding the key into the lock, I opened the door and invited him in.

"I know and I don't blame you, but I need you to hear what I have to say."

"I'm about to make some tea. Would you like some?"

"Only if it's green." He smiled.

"Yeah! My kind of man. Green tea it is."

Eli took a seat at the table while I prepared the tea. There was nothing he could say that would make me change my mind about Sebastian. But I owed him the courtesy of hearing him out.

"Look, I'm not defending him at all, and what he did last night was totally crossing the line, but I know he deeply cares for you."

"He has a funny way of showing it." I poured the water into the cups.

"I'm going to tell you something about him. He's had it rough since the day he was born. He had to fight for everything in his life. He was determined to climb out of the trenches and make something of himself."

"That's no excuse for violence," I spoke as I set his cup of tea down in front of him.

"I agree. Sebastian is a good man and he has a good heart."

"Heart of stone." I interrupted.

"True, but only where women are concerned."

"Why? Did he have an ex-lover that cheated on him or something?"

"No. If only it were that simple. He's never allowed himself to get close to anyone. He's allowed the scars of his past to keep him closed off from everything except his business."

"What happened to him?"

"It's not my place to tell you, but I've known him since we were young boys."

I sighed. "Eli, why are you here? To tell me that he couldn't help punching Corey because of his past?"

"No, Chloe. I'm here to tell you that he really cares for you and you need to reach out to him. I've never seen him like this with anyone before."

"You mean punching people out?"

"No." He smirked. "You've affected him in ways I never thought possible. He's happy when you're around. And that's something I haven't seen very much in his life."

I got up from the table and stood behind the kitchen counter. "Well, he's the one who shut me out and then had the nerve to punch my ex-boyfriend—who's gay, by the way—because we were dancing."

Eli walked over to me and placed his hand on mine.

"Just give it some thought, Chloe. He's a broken man and I do believe you are the only person in this world who can put him back together. If I didn't feel so strongly about that, I wouldn't be here. Thanks for the tea." He turned, and as he started to walk away, he looked back at me. "Please don't ever tell him we had this conversation."

"I won't. I promise."

Chapter 26

Sebastian

Her words kept playing over and over in my mind. "You're a monster. I never want to see you again." The truth was that she was right. I *was* a monster and I let my anger and jealousy get the best of me. I'd never lost control like that before, especially over a woman. I blew it. The best thing that had ever happened to me now hated me. Was she even capable of hate? Her eyes told me everything. That look of hurt, anger, and hatred would be forever etched into my memory. She deserved nothing more than to be happy and I needed to make sure she was. She'd get over what I'd done and she'd get over me. But I wasn't so sure I'd ever get over her. I had ruined her birthday. Fuck, how did I not even know it was her birthday? I should have known. If only I would have opened up to her and told her everything about me, I would have known and things would have been different.

A couple of weeks had passed since that night and every day became harder to deal with. I'd stop outside the window of the gallery and look in with the hopes of just seeing her and making sure she was okay. When she got off work, I'd make Eli follow her with me in the back, just so I knew she made it home and she was safe. Every night, she'd stop and talk to Willie.

Sometimes for a few minutes, and sometimes longer. He wasn't the only homeless man she talked to. There was a group of them that hung out in the alley. Almost as if they were a family and she was a part of it. Their faces lit up every time she'd stop and talk to them.

****

Chloe

Sebastian followed me everywhere I went. I wasn't stupid and I could feel his presence. I guess you could say it was the connection we had. Ever since Eli left my apartment that day, I couldn't stop thinking about what he had said about Sebastian having to fight for everything and climb out of the trenches to make something of himself. My mom told me that Sebastian punching Corey was his way of fighting for me, even though it was wrong.

It was Saturday and I decided to go to Central Park to think. Being outdoors and surrounded by nature always helped me to think more clearly. The work week was extremely busy. Between organizing another exhibition, having dinner with my parents, and visiting with Sienna and Sam, I just needed a day to myself. I felt out of balance, which I was attributing to a man named Sebastian.

I had the cab driver drop me off at the west entrance of the park and I made my way to Shakespeare Garden. It was my favorite spot in all of Central Park because it was quiet and the perfect place to meditate. Walking down the cobblestone path, I admired the beautiful flowers that were in bloom. When I found the perfect spot to settle, I laid out my blanket and set my picnic basket down. I took in a deep cleansing breath and closed my eyes. Taking in the beautiful sounds of nature, I heard something or someone. Opening my eyes, I looked around. Sighing, I closed my eyes and began to meditate. Once again, I heard something.

"Sebastian, I know you're here," I spoke in a loud voice. "And I also know how you've been following me. So just come on out and stop being so damn stalkerish."

"How did you know?" he softly asked as he emerged from behind a tree.

"I just knew. You know when someone is following you."

"I wasn't stalking you, Chloe. I was just making sure you were safe and okay."

"Whatever, Sebastian. Since you followed me out here, you might as well sit down so you can see that I'm okay." I patted the empty spot next to me.

"Are you sure?"

"Yes."

He sat down next to me and I couldn't help but stare at him. He was so handsome but looked so lost.

"What were you doing?" he asked.

"Trying to meditate. You know, you really should try it some time. You could stand to gain some inner peace."

He gave me a frown and I couldn't help but laugh.

"So is that why you do it, to gain inner peace?"

"That and other things. It makes you more grounded so you can live life more in the present."

"Oh. I'm sorry I interrupted you."

"It's fine. Would you like some grapes?" I asked as I reached into the picnic basket and pulled out a small Ziploc bag.

"No. I'm good."

"You don't like grapes?" I cocked my head.

"I like grapes."

"Then why don't you want any?"

"Because I don't." His brow arched.

"Why? There has to be a reason. Aren't you hungry? Even if you weren't hungry, a couple grapes won't hurt you."

"Fine. I'll have some grapes." He smiled as he reached into the bag and took a couple.

"I'm still mad at you," I spoke as I popped a grape into my mouth.

"Then you didn't do enough meditating." He grinned.

Shaking my head, I bit down on my bottom lip. "Trust me, I meditate every day, but you punched my friend for no reason."

"I know and believe me, I will regret what I did until the day I die. I can't apologize to you enough, Chloe. I'm sorry."

I could hear the sincerity in his voice and see the look of regret on his face.

"Fine. Apology accepted." I softly placed my hand on his.

He looked down at our hands and then at me.

"Thank you. It means a lot to me. Chloe, there's something else I need to talk to you about."

"What is it?" I asked nervously.

He looked away. "It can never work between us."

"Why do you say that?" My heart started to ache.

"Because I could never give you what you need and deserve. You were right when you called me a monster. That's exactly what I am."

"No, Sebastian. I was angry. I didn't mean it."

"Whether you did or not, it's what I am." He removed his hand from mine. "I don't want to make this harder than it already is." He stood up and stared straight ahead. He couldn't even look at me.

Suddenly, I felt a rain drop hit my hand.

"I better go. I'm sorry, Chloe. All I want is for you to be happy and being with me will make you more miserable." He turned and began to walk away.

"Have you always been a coward?" I shouted as the rain started to come down.

"Excuse me? It's really raining now. We should go seek shelter."

"No. I'm staying right here. How many storms are you hiding from, Sebastian?" I asked as I stood up and stared at him.

"What are you talking about? Chloe, it's raining and we're getting soaked. We can talk about this somewhere else."

"Have you ever heard the quote: Life isn't about waiting for the storm to pass; it's about learning to dance in the rain?"

"For God sakes, Chloe," he shouted.

"If you wait for every storm to pass, you'll waste time, and then you'll have nothing to show for it, past or present. Your first reaction when it started raining was to run and hide from it. Why?"

"Chloe, I'm serious. I have no clue what you're talking about. All I know is that we're both standing out here, soaking wet!" he yelled.

"Tell me what you're so afraid of, Sebastian! What happened to you?"

"Nothing. This is how I am! I'm not capable of emotion. I don't cry and I certainly can't love you the way you deserve to be loved!"

"Why? You saying you can't isn't good enough. There's a reason you feel that way."

He ran his hands through his hair as I watched him struggle to find the words.

"Tell me, Sebastian!" I yelled as loud as I could.

"You want to know why?!" he shouted as he walked towards me. "Because I don't know how to love! I have never been loved by anyone my entire life. How do you give love when you never received it?!"

"What about your parents?"

"I never knew my parents."

I nearly lost my breath hearing him speak those words. Everything began to make sense now. I walked closer to where he was standing. Wrapping my arms around his neck, I hugged him tight. It took a few moments, but he finally wrapped his arms around me. Slowly, we both sank to the ground as the rain poured down on us.

"I don't want to lose you, Chloe. You're the first person in my life that has meant something to me. But it frightens me to be with you."

"I don't want to lose you either and there's no reason to be frightened."

He broke our embrace and his eyes stared into mine.

"You deserve so much better."

"I think that's up to me to decide." I smiled. "I know what I need and what I need is you."

His mouth smashed into mine with such passion it sent me into another world. I'd missed him and his touch.

"If we're going to do this, you can't keep things from me." I placed my hand on his face.

"I know and I will tell you everything. I promise."

Smiling, I spoke, "How about we go back to my place and get out of these wet clothes?"

"I don't have any dry clothes at your place."

"Who said you need clothes? Clothing is totally optional at my place." I grinned as I pressed my forehead against his.

"I think I like your place." He smiled as he brushed his lips against mine.

We stood up, grabbed the blanket and the picnic basket, and headed to his limo. After climbing in, Sebastian grabbed my hand.

"How about we go to my place instead? I have plenty of t-shirts that would look adorable on you. Clothing is optional, of course. Plus, I have this huge bathtub that I think you'll fall in love with."

"Is it big enough for two?" I asked.

"It's big enough for four."

I smiled. "I think I like your place." I leaned over and kissed him.

"Good. Because you'll be spending a lot of time there."

"Promise?"

He brought his thumb to my lips. "I promise."

Glancing up, Eli gave me a wink through the rearview mirror. This was the start of something good—hell, something great—but Sebastian was going to take a lot of work.

Chapter 27

Sebastian

I felt like a weight had been lifted off my shoulders. I still had to tell her everything, but that didn't matter to me anymore. I wanted to tell her. I needed to tell her. Holding her hand, we stepped into the elevator and took it up to my penthouse. As much as I wanted to rip her clothes off and fuck her into oblivion, I had to take things slow. Telling her about my past was first priority as far as I was concerned.

Stepping into the penthouse, I led her to my bedroom and grabbed a t-shirt from the drawer.

"If you'll give me your clothes, I'll throw them in the dryer."

"So are you going to show me that big bathtub of yours?" she asked with a grin as she stripped out of her clothes.

"It's right through here." I led the way.

"Ah. It's beautiful." She reached over and started the water.

"You're taking a bath now?"

"*We* are taking a bath. I need your naked body to warm me up."

"We should talk first, Chloe," I spoke with seriousness.

"And we will. In the bathtub."

"I don't want to have sex until you know everything."

She frowned. "Who said anything about sex? I said a bath."

"But I won't be able to control myself with your naked body against me. You know my cock won't behave."

"I like it when your cock misbehaves. Now get out of those wet clothes and get in the tub."

Fuck. Staring at her naked body as she climbed into the tub sent my dick straight up in seconds without warning. I missed her and her sexy body. Stripping out of my clothes as fast as I could, I climbed in behind her and tightly wrapped her in my arms.

"I know this is hard for you, Sebastian, so I'll start. How come you never knew your parents?" she asked as she ran her finger up and down my arm.

"They left me on the steps of a church in Minneapolis when I was a week old with a note that said: 'please take care of our son and find him a good home.' A woman who worked at the church took me in and took care of me until I was three years old. She was older and died of a massive heart attack in her sleep. I then became the property of the State of Minnesota. I was in and out of numerous foster homes until I was ten years old, all of which were very bad situations. After the last foster home I was taken away from, I was put in a group home. That's where I met Eli."

"I don't understand? You were never adopted?"

"No. The system was fucked up, Chloe. It's not as bad now as it was all those years ago, but still. I had some problems and nobody wanted to adopt a kid that old who they considered trouble."

"What kind of problems?"

I took in a deep breath. "I was a very angry child. I went into fits of rages, stole, drank, broke curfew, got arrested, and when I was sixteen, I was kicked out after smashing three of the windows in the house. They considered me an adult and sent me out into the world to live like one."

"My God, Sebastian. Did you go to school?"

"Yeah. That was one area in life that I was really smart in. Even with everything I had been through, I always went to school and got good grades. When the group home kicked me out, I still went to school every day."

"Where did you live?"

"In an abandoned house tucked away down a dirt road that nobody ever traveled on."

"How did you live? What did you do for money?"

"I had some money working odd jobs while I was at the group home. Then, when I was kicked out, I worked for a man named Kurtis. He owned a small construction company. I worked for him every day after school and all day on Saturdays. He knew of my situation and he took a chance on me. He told me that if I screwed up, not only would he cut off my balls, but he'd make sure I never got another job in town. He was kind of scary." I smiled. "I remember the first time he came to my house. He looked around and told me that I didn't have to live like that. He said to use what skills he was teaching me and fix the place up. I asked him if he would help me and he told me no."

"Why? That was awfully rude of him."

"He said that it was something I needed to do on my own."

"So did you?"

"Yep. I worked on it after I did my homework at night and all day Sundays. I can't even explain how I felt once it was finished."

"How long did it take you?"

"Two years. I even redid the outside. I tore out bushes, chopped down a few trees, put up a white picket fence, and poured a new driveway."

"How on earth did you learn to do all that?"

"I studied and did a lot of research. Plus, I knew a few people in the trade who gave me some tips."

"Remodeling a house is very expensive."

"Kurtis let me use a lot of the leftovers from the job sites and I would go to the scrap yard a lot and collect things. It kept me out of trouble."

"Kurtis must have been so proud of you. What did he say when he saw the house?"

"He never saw the house. About six months before the house was finished, he was diagnosed with lung cancer and was given a couple of months to live. He knew what he had but refused to go to the doctor. One day, he collapsed and ended up in the hospital. I remember standing at his bedside and him saying to me, "Son, you go get the deed to that house in your name. When it's finished, sell it. You'll make a killing off of it and all your hard work would have paid off. Take the money and get yourself settled somewhere. Make something of yourself. He gave me the name of his lawyer in case I had any trouble and then he passed away that night."

****

Chloe

I couldn't stop the tears from filling my eyes as Sebastian told his story. What he had been through as a child was heartbreaking. Turning my body around so I was facing him, I ran my hand down his cheek.

"I'm so sorry. That must have been very hard on you when he passed away."

"I couldn't cry, Chloe. All I knew was that I was so angry at him for dying. I finished the house, graduated from high school, and sold it with the help of a realtor. I made a shitload of money."

"Now I'm sure that's just nickel and dime to you." I smiled.

"Yeah. It is." He scrunched up his nose.

"So then what happened?" I asked as I laid my head on his chest.

"I bought another rundown house, fixed it up, sold it, and made a lot of money. I kept on doing that, and when I was twenty years old, I made my first million. When I was twenty-one, I made two million, and that's when I moved here to New York and started Bennett Industries out the apartment I lived in."

"And you did that all by yourself?"

"Yeah. With a little help from Eli. Like I said, we had met in the group home. He was taken away from his parents when he was ten years old because they were heavy drug users. He was the only friend I made and that's because he was just as bad as I was. He was sent back to his parents when he was fifteen. They moved here to New York, but we still kept in touch almost every day."

"So that's why you moved here? Because of Eli?"

"Pretty much. I threw ideas at him and he encouraged me to make the move. Plus, the housing market here was on an upswing."

"How did he become your driver?"

"He just wasn't cut out for the business world and he knew it. But being my best friend, I had to do something. So I bought him a limo and hired him as my personal driver. I pay him very well and he's happy. Once I started Bennett Industries and had a few more sold houses under my belt, I looked into businesses that were failing. I figured if I could do it with houses, I could do with businesses. I made connections with people, wined and dined them, and learned to play the game. I bought a company that was nearly bankrupt, brought in a team to help me get it back up and running, which cost me a lot of money, and then I sold it for more money than I ever imagined. And that's what led me to be where I am today."

"You had to be happy about that?" I asked as I turned back around and snuggled against him.

"About the company, yes. About the obscene amount of money I made, yes. But I was still that angry boy whose parents abandoned him. I had no control over what happened to me back when I was a child, but when I was kicked out of the group home, I was free and I took control over my life and vowed never to let anyone try to control my life again."

I reached up and kissed his lips. "I have more questions, but we need to get out of this tub."

He chuckled. "Okay. Let me help you out."

Sebastian climbed out first and wrapped a towel around his waist. Holding out a towel for me, he grabbed my hand and helped me, wrapping the towel around my body.

"I think your cock bruised my back. All that hardness pushing against me."

His brow arched as he turned me around, lifted up the towel, and examined my back.

"I don't see any bruises. But maybe I should take a closer look just to be sure."

I shivered as he softly ran his tongue along my back, licking up and down my spine with long, smooth strokes. He placed his hand between my legs and cupped me down below. I swear I almost had an orgasm. When he dipped his finger inside me, I gasped. Fuck, he felt so good. My knees felt weak in anticipation for what was coming. He stood up, his finger exploring my insides as his hot breath trailed across my neck.

"Does your back feel better?" he whispered.

"Uh huh." I let out a low moan.

"I've missed you so much, and I've missed this."

"Me too," I spoke breathlessly.

I let the towel drop as he picked me up and set me on the bathroom counter, kissing me passionately.

"I can't wait any longer. I need to be inside you right now."

He pulled my hips forward and I wrapped my legs around him, forcing the towel off his hips.

"I can't wait either."

He thrust inside me and we both moaned. My insides were on fire with pleasure as he slowly moved in and out. Our eyes locked on each other's as passion ignited within us.

"You are so beautiful." His lips trailed across my neck.

"So are you." My hands raked through his hair as I swelled around him.

He gasped as he lifted me off the counter and carried me to the bed. Laying me down, his thrusting became faster as he hovered over me and his mouth explored my breasts. Moans between us grew louder as my body reached its peak and I fell into a cosmic orgasm.

"Uh. Fuck, baby," he moaned as his thrusting slowed and he exploded inside me.

"Uh," I moaned with him in pure ecstasy.

Sebastian lowered his head and brushed his lips against mine before collapsing on top of me.

"Are you okay?" I lightly laughed.

"I'm fine. I'm just paralyzed at the moment," he mumbled against my neck.

"Oh good. That makes two of us."

Chapter 28

Chloe

As I slipped into one of Sebastian's t-shirts, he pulled on a pair of sweatpants and we went down to the kitchen to grab something to eat.

"Well, it doesn't appear there's much in here. How about we order in? What are you in the mood for?" he asked as he placed his hands on my hips and kissed my forehead.

"It doesn't matter. Whatever you're in the mood for is fine."

"It doesn't matter, Chloe. It's up to you."

"Chinese?"

"Sounds good. There's a place that delivers a couple of blocks over."

After placing our order, Sebastian grabbed a bottle of wine while I took a seat at the island.

"Thank you, Sebastian," I spoke.

"For what, baby?" he asked as he poured the wine.

"For telling me about your past."

He gave me a small smile as he handed me the glass. "It felt good to tell you."

"I still have some more questions." I bit down on my bottom lip.

"What do you want to know?"

"Why relationships were off the table for you?"

He took in a sharp breath. "Because of the person I am, Chloe. What I experienced, how I grew up, everything. I want to be very honest with you." His fingers brushed away some strands of hair from my forehead. "This. Us. It's still very hard for me. What I'm doing is very new to me and I'm scared."

"What are you scared of?"

"I'm scared of letting you down or not being good enough for you. I'm scared of not being there for you emotionally. It's something I have to work on. I care about you, Chloe, and I don't want to lose you."

Standing up from the stool, I reached up and wrapped my arms around him. On the outside he was a confident man who stood tall and proud at what he'd accomplished, but on the inside, he was still a frightened, unloved little boy.

"You have nothing to be scared of, Sebastian. When you care about someone, everything else comes naturally. You are more than good enough for me and I don't ever want to hear you say that again. Okay?"

The doorbell rang, so Sebastian kissed my head and went to answer it. Picking up my phone from the counter, I facetimed Sienna since I missed three calls from her and a text message saying: *"You better be having great sex or dead."*

"It's about fucking time. Wait. Where are you? That's not your apartment."

"I'm at Sebastian's." I smiled.

"Why? Wait a minute. What are you wearing? Jesus, Chloe, did you two have sex?"

"It's a long story, but." I smiled. "We are officially dating."

"As in a relationship?"

"Yes. I have to go; he's coming."

"I bet he is." She grinned.

"Shut up. I'll call you tomorrow."

Sebastian walked into the kitchen with the bag of food and set it on the counter.

"Did I hear you talking to someone?" he asked.

"Yeah. I called Sienna since she called me three times and sent a text message."

"It seems like you two are glued at the hip." He smiled.

"We are. She's more or less my sister. We share everything. So." I got up from the stool and ran my finger down his chest. "If you date me, you're getting her too."

"Ah. Does she do threesomes?" He winked.

"Actually, she does."

His eyes widened. "I was kidding."

"I'm not." I shrugged.

"By the way, I want to thank you," he spoke as he took the cartons of food to the table.

"For what?"

"If I would have invested in that company, I would have lost millions. But thanks to you and Venus, I didn't."

"What happened?"

"Apparently, they had made a bad business decision they failed to tell me about when we were negotiating the contract."

"Oh. Idiots."

"Yes. Complete idiots."

"I'm glad I could help. If you ever have any more questions about the retrogrades, just let me know."

He chuckled. "I will."

After we ate, Sebastian grabbed the bottle of wine and our glasses and we went to the bedroom where we spent the rest of the night making love.

****

Sebastian

What a beautiful way to start a Sunday morning. As I lay there, watching her sleep, my mind was reeling with ways to make up her birthday to her. I wanted to take her on another trip, but I wasn't sure if she could get the time off work. I wanted to whisk her away somewhere beautiful and make a memory that neither one of us would ever forget.

She stirred and opened her eyes. She lifted her head from my chest and looked at me with a smile.

"Good morning," she whispered.

"Good morning. Did you sleep well?"

"I did. And you?" She ran her finger across my lips.

"Very well."

She laid her head back down on my chest as I tightened my arm around her.

"Oh shit!" she exclaimed as she sat up quickly.

"What?"

"Today is my parents' anniversary party. Would you like to come with me?" She grinned.

"How long have they been married?" I asked out of curiosity.

"Oh, they aren't married." She cocked her head.

"Huh?" I asked in confusion.

"They never felt the need to validate their love by a piece of paper."

"I see. So this anniversary is what?"

"Twenty-six years together. Say you'll come."

I wasn't very comfortable around a family setting, but I could tell that it meant a lot to her. So I agreed to go.

"Thank you. You won't regret it. Or you might. But it'll be fun." She leaned over and kissed my lips.

Pulling her on top of me, I pushed my hard cock against her.

"Feel that?" I asked.

She flashed a beautiful smile.

"It needs to be taken care of before we get out of this bed for the day." I winked.

"Oh really?" She reached her hand down and stroked me with her slender fingers.

"Fuck, Chloe." I shuddered.

"Come on, big boy. Show me what you got."

Rolling her on her back, I hovered over her. She had just unleashed the beast inside me.

Chapter 29

Chloe

"Hey, Eli." I smiled as I walked into the kitchen.

"Hello, Chloe. I was happy to get Sebastian's call about driving you home. I take it the two of you are—"

"Oh yeah." I bit down on my bottom lip and smiled. "We certainly are."

He chuckled. "Where is he?"

"In the shower. He told me everything last night."

"Good. I'm glad to hear that."

"Glad to hear what?" Sebastian asked as he walked into the kitchen.

"Just that the two of you are together," Eli replied.

Sebastian placed his hands on my hips.

"Eli is going to drive you home and then I'll be by later to pick you up for your parents' party. I have an errand to run."

"What kind of errand? I can go with you?"

"No, no. You'd be bored. I'll see you later." He kissed my lips and walked out.

"Huh. What's he up to?" I narrowed my eye at Eli.

He shrugged. "I have no idea, but I wouldn't question him. Are you ready to go?"

Stepping inside my apartment, I set down my purse and took a shower to start getting ready for the party. I was a little worried about what Sebastian would think of my parents' friends. This wasn't the type of party he was used to attending. There would be no fancy dresses, beautiful lighting, expensive champagne, fine food, or expensive table linens. Just a bunch of rowdy people who liked to party barefoot, listen to folk music, drink the cheapest beer money can buy, and smoke a little weed.

I had just finished putting on my makeup and styling my hair when a text message from Sebastian came through.

"I'm downstairs. Buzz me in."

My heart fluttered. Even though it had only been a few hours, I already missed him. As he walked up the stairs, he whistled when he saw me standing at door.

"You look so sexy." He smiled as he kissed me.

"Mhm. So do you." I wrapped my arms around him. "Come on in. Did you get your errand done?" I asked as I headed to the bedroom.

"I sure did." He followed behind. "I have something for you."

"For me?" I smiled. "Why?"

"Happy belated birthday, baby." He handed me a small blue square box from Tiffany's.

"Sebastian." I pouted. "You didn't have to get me anything."

"Yes I did. Now don't argue. Open it."

I untied the pretty blue bow and carefully removed the lid.

"Oh, Sebastian." Tears started to form in my eyes as I looked at the beautiful 18kt rose gold bracelet with a heart charm that displayed the letter "C" in diamonds. "This is gorgeous." I took it out of the box and held it up.

"Do you really like it?"

"I love it. Wow. Thank you." I brushed my lips against his.

"You're welcome. Let me help you put it on."

He took the bracelet from me and clasped it around my wrist.

"It looks beautiful on you."

"You have excellent taste, Mr. Bennett. My wrist thanks you."

He let out a low growl as his lips traveled to my ear and his hand slipped up my short, silk robe.

"Is that the only part of your body that thanks me? Because my hand seems to think otherwise."

I let out a gasp as his finger plunged inside me.

"Every part of my body wants to thank you in every way possible, but we don't have time right now."

His lips hovered over mine. "Baby, all we need is a few minutes. Take your pick. The bed, the wall, the floor; it's up to you."

He had me in a trance as his finger explored me and his hot breath swept over my face. His sultry eyes stared into mine with such passion that I couldn't resist him. My hands reached down and undid his pants, sliding them off his hips while he untied my robe and pushed it off my shoulders.

"The wall." I smiled.

"You have clearly read my mind." He picked me up.

As I wrapped my legs around his waist, he pushed my back up against the wall and pushed himself inside me, hard and deep. Moans escaped my lips as subtle grunts escaped his with each hard thrust. It didn't take long for us to reach our peak and release ourselves to each other.

****

When we stepped inside my parents' apartment, they welcomed us with open arms.

"Happy anniversary, parents." I smiled as I hugged them.

"Thank you, pumpkin." My dad smiled and then turned his attention to Sebastian. "Nice to see you again, Sebastian." He extended his hand.

"Likewise, Larry. Happy anniversary."

My mom placed her hands on each side of Sebastian's face. "Thank you for coming." She smiled.

"It's my pleasure."

After introducing Sebastian to my parents' friends, my dad strummed his guitar to get everyone's attention.

"I would like to say a few words. Twenty-six years ago today, I met the woman of my dreams. She was and still is the most beautiful woman in the world."

"Oh, Larry." My mom smiled as she stood next to him.

He turned to her and took hold of both her hands. "I love you, Ophelia, and these past twenty-six years have been incredible to share with you. The best part of all these years is the beautiful gift you gave me: our daughter, Chloe."

Tears sprang to my eyes as I sat there and listened to my dad.

"I just want you to know that I can't wait to spend another twenty-six years plus with you. You are my shining star and I love you."

As I wiped a tear from my eye, Sebastian put his arm around me. My parents embraced each other tightly as everyone in the room cheered.

"Chloe," my dad spoke as he handed me his guitar, "the song we discussed."

With a smile, I got up, grabbed his guitar, and began to play "Only You" by Joshua Radin. Sebastian stood across the room and intently watched me as I sang with my father while the love my parents had for each other radiated throughout the room.

After the party was over, I stayed back to help my mom clean up.

"Chloe, I don't want you to help. You go home with Sebastian. I'm sure the two of you are dying to have sex." She smiled.

"I'm good, Mom. We had sex all morning and right before we came."

Sebastian's jaw dropped as he looked over at me.

"Oh, Sebastian, don't be embarrassed. I think it's wonderful the two of you are together and having so much sex. It's nothing to be ashamed of. The cohabitation between two people who love each other is a beautiful and nurturing thing."

Ah shit, she had to throw in the L word. I could tell by the look on Sebastian's face that what she said bothered him, so I decided to listen to her and head home. As we were driving home, Sebastian made a comment that caught me off guard.

"I think what your parents are doing is great."

"Which thing are you speaking of?" I asked.

"The whole relationship thing without marriage. I mean, who needs that stupid piece of paper to be with someone for the rest of your life? If you're happy with the way things are, why change it? Like they say, if it isn't broken, don't try to fix it."

"I don't know. I kind of disagree, but don't tell them that."

"What do you mean you disagree?"

"Marriage is the ultimate level of commitment. I think it's too easy for people just to break up or walk away if they hit a bump in the road. It allows you to be fully committed to one person. I don't know, Sebastian. I just believe in the whole concept of marriage."

"Your parents seem happy with the way things are."

"Maybe they are, but I'm not. I'm still waiting for them to take it to the next level. But I know they never will, and in a way, I'm disappointed about it."

"Well, I think it's great and I like the way they think," he spoke.

I was getting irritated and I wanted the subject dropped. He was trying to be subtle to let me know that marriage would never be an option. Was I okay with that? I wasn't sure. It was too early in our relationship to even think that far ahead.

I patted his arm. "I'm glad you like them."

He gave me a small smile and kissed my head.

Chapter 30

Sebastian

Three Months Later…

The past three months with Chloe had been the best three months of my entire life. I took her to Hawaii for a week to celebrate her birthday properly. It was just the two of us, sipping drinks, lying on the beach, having sinful amounts of sex, and exploring the beautiful sights Hawaii had to offer. We took turns staying at each other's apartments. I had some of my things at her place and she had some of her things at mine. Life couldn't be better. When she wasn't around, I felt empty inside. I missed her every single minute of the day she wasn't with me.

While I was sitting in my office, Damien walked in.

"Take a look at this and tell me if you think this would be a wise investment." He handed me a manila folder and took a seat across from me.

As I was reviewing the contents inside, Damien spoke, "Things seem to be going pretty good with you and Chloe."

"Yeah. They are." I smiled as I looked up at him.

"Have you told her that you love her yet?"

I arched my brow at him, wondering why he was asking.

"No. Why?"

"Just wondering." He shrugged. "Has she told you?"

"Yeah. She's said it a few times."

"And how do you respond?"

"I give her a smile and say 'me too.'"

He rolled his eyes. "Come on, Sebastian. Really?"

"I don't need to say it. She knows I do."

"Obviously, you need a lesson in Romance 101. If you love someone, you want to tell her every day. I tell Lina that I love her all the time. Women need to hear those words. It validates the relationship."

"That's you. I'm just not comfortable saying it and our relationship doesn't need validation."

"And how long do you think Chloe will accept that? What if something happened to her and you never told her you loved her?"

I sighed. "Enough talk about me and Chloe, Damien. This company has potential, but I need more information." I handed him back the file.

He took it from me and got up from his seat. "Sorry, Sebastian. I just think Chloe is the best thing that's happened to you and you need to make sure you hang on to her." He walked out of my office.

I did love her and she knew it, or at least I thought she did, but I found it hard to say the words. Not because I didn't love her, but because I had never spoken those words to anyone before. Were they really necessary? Just like having a piece of paper to validate your relationship or commitment to each other? Picking up my phone, I sent her a text message.

"Hi. I was just sitting here thinking about you."

"Hey, you. I'm thinking about you too. I miss you."

"I miss you more, baby. I'll see you later."

"Can't wait. I love you."

"Me too."

I sighed as I stared at the last words I sent her. Why was it so hard for me to tell her?

****

Chloe

"Is that Loverboy?" Sienna asked as we sat and ate lunch.

"Yes." I grinned.

"Has he said the big 'L' word yet?"

"No. Whenever I tell him that I love him, he always replies with 'me too.' It's really starting to bother me a little."

"Tell his dumb ass that." She took a bite of her salad.

Waving my hand in front of my face, I spoke, "Nah. I don't want to start a fight or anything. He'll eventually come around and tell me."

"What? Did you just hear yourself? The two of you are in a hot and heavy relationship. He's taken you on trips, given you expensive jewelry, and you have sex twice a day."

"Sometimes three." I held up three fingers.

"The point is, Chloe, he should have said it by now."

"He will." I smiled. "When the time is right."

"You are too forgiving of a person."

After finishing lunch, Sienna went back to work and I headed to the art gallery. Climbing out of the cab, I saw Willie walking down the street.

"Hey, Willie," I yelled and gave him a wave.

He stopped and waited for me.

"Hey, Chloe." He coughed.

"Are you okay?"

"Yeah. Just a little cold, nothing to worry about." He coughed again.

"Okay. You better take care of yourself. I'll stop by and see you soon. I have to get back to work." I smiled.

I couldn't stop thinking about Willie and how he didn't look so good. After work, I ran to the drugstore and picked up some cough drops, a few bottles of water, and some cold medicine.

"I bought you some medicine, Willie." I held up the plastic bag as he sat up against the brick wall in the alley.

"Chloe, you didn't have to do that."

"Don't be silly. You're not feeling well and you need to take care of yourself. I also picked up your favorite candy bar."

"You're too good to me. Thank you."

"You're welcome. I have to go. Sebastian and I are going out and I have to get home and change."

"It makes me happy to see you so happy." He smiled.

"I *am* happy. See you later, Willie." I waved.

As I walked up to my building, Eli pulled up and Sebastian climbed out of the limo.

"Are you just getting home?" he asked as he gave me a kiss.

"Yeah. I stopped by the drugstore after work and picked up some cold medicine for Willie. He's not feeling well."

"Ah. That was nice of you."

"It won't take me long to change. If you can behave yourself, I may even let you watch." I grinned as I grabbed his tie and he followed behind.

"Oh, I'm going to watch, but I can't guarantee that I'll behave. I can't seem to do that when I'm around you."

After a nice dinner and a bottle of wine, we headed back to Sebastian's penthouse. Lying in bed, his arms held me as my head lay on his muscular chest. This was where I belonged.

"Hey, Sebastian," I spoke as I stroked his chest.

"Hmm?" he spoke.

"I love you."

For a moment, there was silence and I thought for sure he was mustering up the courage to say it back.

"Me too, baby." He kissed the top of my head. "Now get some sleep."

A tiny piece of my heart broke when I heard him say that. Was I expecting too much from him too soon? Maybe I shouldn't have been so free to tell him that I loved him when I did. I'd never forget the look on his face. We were in Hawaii and we were having dinner on the beach. The sun was setting and it was a magical moment; one of those moments that take your breath away. It was romantic and I got caught up in the scenery. But it was a moment that I would never regret. Telling him that I loved him made me incredibly happy. I wanted him to know because he had never been loved his whole life. But the more I said it, the deeper the cut in my soul became because he couldn't bring himself to say it back. Closing my eyes, I tried to push it out of my mind. Tomorrow was a new day, and maybe, just maybe, it would be the day that he would tell me that he loved me too.

Chapter 31

Chloe

Two Weeks Later

I picked up the white stick that sat on the bathroom counter for the past five minutes. Holding it in my hand, tears started to fill my eyes as I stared at the blue plus sign displayed in the window. With a smile, I looked at my mom.

"We're having a baby!"

Chapter 32

Sebastian

On the way to Chloe's, I had Eli stop at the florist, where I picked up a dozen gerbera daisies in multiple colors. There was much celebrating to do tonight because I had just signed a deal that made my company millions of dollars. I wanted to take her out to celebrate, but she insisted on cooking me dinner. Which was fine. Just being with her was celebratory enough.

When I stepped into her apartment, she greeted me with a hug and a passionate kiss, congratulating me on the deal.

"Sebastian, you brought me daisies." She smiled. "But I should be giving you something."

Following her into the kitchen, I spoke, "Trust me, baby, you will be giving me something after dinner." I winked.

She seemed to be in an exceptional mood. Don't get me wrong, she was always in a good mood, but tonight, she seemed different. Opening the bottle of wine that was sitting on the counter, I poured some into two glasses and set them on the table. Halfway through dinner, I excused myself to the bathroom.

While I was standing there taking a piss, my eyes happened to glance down at the small trashcan that sat next to the toilet. Reaching down, I pulled out the white stick that displayed a positive sign and my heart started racing out of control. Sweat formed on my forehead and I found it difficult to catch my breath. Pulling the box out of the trash, I read the words: EPT. Shock overtook my body as my hands started to shake. Throwing the box and the stick back in the trash, I shut the lid to the toilet and sat down, cupping my face in my hands. Chloe was pregnant and I didn't know what to do. Was I happy about it? Hell no. I didn't want kids. Not now, not ever. How the fuck did this happen? Chloe was on the pill. Did she do this on purpose? All kinds of crazy thoughts went through my head. Standing up, I took in a deep breath, grabbed my phone from my pocket, and calmly walked back to the table.

"I'm sorry, Chloe, but I have to go."

"What? Why? What's wrong?" she asked as she stood up.

"I just got a call from Damien. Something about the deal and he needs me to come to the office. I'm sorry."

"Okay. Will you be coming back?"

"Probably not. I don't know how long this is going to take and it could go really late. I'll text you later." I kissed her head and bolted out the door.

Walking down the street, I called Eli.

"Yes, Sebastian?"

"Come get me. I'm around the block from Chloe's apartment."

"What? Why?"

"Just hurry up, Eli." I ended the call.

As I stood with my back up against the wall of Pizzapopolous, dazed and confused, I heard someone call my name.

"Sebastian?" Connor smiled.

"Oh. Hey, Connor. Ellery."

"What are you doing just standing here like this?"

"Waiting for Eli."

"Where's Chloe?" Ellery asked.

"She's at home. We were in the middle of eating dinner when I got a call from Damien. I have to go into the office," I spoke nervously.

"Ah. I hate those kinds of calls." Connor smiled. "Well, good seeing you, my friend. Let's have dinner one night; the four of us."

"Sure." I gave him a nod. "You two have a good night."

Finally, Eli pulled up and I wasted no time climbing into the backseat.

"What's going on? Are you not feeling well? You look kind of pale."

"I don't know." I stared straight ahead.

"Sebastian, what's wrong? Did you and Chloe have a fight?"

A fight. If only it were that simple. Taking in a deep breath, I looked at Eli.

"Chloe's pregnant."

His eyes instantly darted to the rearview mirror.

"What?"

"I was going to the bathroom and I found the pregnancy test in the trash. It was positive."

"So she didn't tell you?"

"No. She didn't get a chance. As soon as I saw it, I made up an excuse that Damien called and needed me at the office."

"You just ran out on her like that?"

"I had to get out of there, Eli."

"What are you going to do?"

"I don't know. I haven't even been able to tell her that I love her, let alone be a father to a kid."

"Be careful, Sebastian." He slowly shook his head.

"Careful is what I thought we were being. For fuck sake, she's on the pill. How the fuck did this happen?"

"I'm not surprised, with the way you two fuck like rabbits. Maybe she missed one or something. I've heard of it happening. People getting pregnant while on birth control."

"I can't be something I'm not. I swear, if she did this on purpose…"

"Oh come on, Sebastian. Chloe would never do something like that."

"I don't know."

Eli pulled up to my building and followed me up to the penthouse. Pouring us a drink, I spoke, "I think I need to get out of town for a while and clear my head. I need to figure things out."

"And what are you going to tell Chloe?"

"That I have an emergency business meeting."

"Lies are not good, Sebastian. They always come back to bite you in the ass. What you need to do is let her tell you that she's pregnant and the two of you need to talk about it."

"I can't. I'm in shock and I need to leave town for a while." I threw back my drink and pulled out my phone, dialing my pilot.

"Hello, Mr. Bennett."

"Make sure the plane is ready tomorrow morning. I'm going to Seattle. I'll be at the airport at eight a.m."

"Sure thing, Mr. Bennett."

Finishing the last sip of my drink, I set my glass down on the bar.

"Be here tomorrow at seven o'clock," I spoke to Eli.

"I don't think you're doing the right thing."

"I don't care what you think!" I shouted. "I need to clear my head."

He put his hands up. "It's your life, Sebastian. It always has been. I'll see you in the morning." He walked out with an attitude.

I waited a couple of hours before I sent Chloe a text message.

"Hi. Listen, I need to fly out tomorrow morning for an emergency meeting in Seattle. I'll be gone at least a week, maybe a little longer."

"Oh. Okay. I'll miss you. There was something I wanted to tell you tonight, but it can wait until you get back."

"Okay. I'll be in touch."

"I love you, Sebastian."

My heart sank as I read her last text message. I didn't respond. I couldn't. I grabbed the suitcase from my closet and began to pack. Once I was finished, I called Damien.

"What's up?" he answered.

"I'm heading to Seattle tomorrow and I'll be gone at least a week, if not longer. You are to oversee the company. This stays between us, Damien."

"Why are you going to Seattle?"

"I just am and I don't want to be bothered while I'm there unless it's serious."

"Okay. Is Chloe going with you?"

"No. I'm going alone and I don't want to discuss it any further. Just do as I ask."

"Okay, Sebastian, but I will admit you have me a little worried."

"There's nothing to worry about. I'll be in touch." I ended the call before he had a chance to say anything.

Chapter 33

Chloe

Two days had passed and I hadn't heard a word from Sebastian. After sending him a few text messages with no response, I tried to call him, only for his phone to go straight to voicemail. Sitting at my desk and rereading his text messages from that night, a nervous feeling flooded my belly. When I told him that I loved him, he didn't even respond with a "me too." Nor did he tell me that he missed me. Something was off with him and it bothered me a great deal. When I dialed Sienna, she answered and held up her finger, telling me to hold on a sec.

"What's up, buttercup?" She smiled.

"Can you come over tonight? I need to talk to you."

"Sure thing. Hey, are you okay?" She frowned.

"I don't really know. We'll talk later."

"Okay. I'll stop and pick us up a pizza on the way over."

I gave her a small smile. "Sounds good. I'll have the wine or tequila waiting."

"Shit, Chloe. Tequila? Did something happen with Sebastian?"

"I'm not sure. I have to go. I'll see you later."

"Okay. Bye." She pouted as she ended the call.

Trying to keep as busy as possible, the work day finally ended and I headed home. Stepping into my apartment, I set my purse down and went into the bedroom to change. Sitting down on the bed, I glanced at the pile of change that sat upon it from Sebastian. I missed him and I couldn't help this gnawing feeling inside me that something was wrong. After changing into my sweatpants and a tank top, I buzzed up Sienna and watched as she walked up the steps with a pizza box and a brown bag in her hand.

"What did you bring?" I asked as I took the pizza box from her.

"I get the impression comfort food is in order, so I stopped at the store and picked up some cookie dough ice cream and a dozen cupcakes from your favorite bakery."

"Aw, thanks."

She followed me into the kitchen and put the ice cream in the freezer.

"So tell me what's going on?"

Taking down two plates, I took them to the table.

"I haven't heard from Sebastian in two days."

"Well, maybe he's really busy and hasn't had a chance to call you."

"Too busy to send his girlfriend a text before he goes to bed at night? I tried calling him and it appears his phone is turned off."

"Huh?" She twisted her face. "Why would he turn off his phone?"

"I don't know. Something isn't right, Sienna." I took a bite of my pizza and threw the slice on the plate, pushing it away. "I don't feel like eating right now."

"Okay. Let's go back to the night he was over for dinner. You said that Damien called him and said that he needed him back at the office."

"Yes, and then he texted me a couple of hours later saying that he needed to fly to Seattle for an emergency meeting and that he'd be gone for at least a week if not longer."

"Why wouldn't he call you and tell you that? I would think that was something he would want to tell you over the phone, not via text."

"I really didn't think anything about it. But I told him that I loved him and he didn't respond back at all."

"If you want my honest opinion," she spoke as she chewed her food, "I think he has a multiple personality disorder."

I sighed as I rolled my eyes. "He does not."

"Eat your pizza. I have to go to the bathroom." She pushed my plate towards me. "If you don't eat your dinner, you can't have any ice cream." She grinned.

Picking up my pizza, I took a small bite and slowly chewed it as I thought about Sebastian. A few moments later, Sienna walked back to the table.

"Umm, Chloe."

I glanced up at her as she stood there holding the pregnancy stick in her hand.

"You said that Sebastian went to the bathroom in the middle of dinner. I think I found the reason he ran out of here so fast." She held up the stick.

My eyes widened and my heart started racing. "Oh my God, he thinks I'm pregnant." I placed my hand over my mouth.

"I would say so. You hadn't told him yet that your mom is pregnant?"

"No. I didn't have a chance to. We were talking about that business deal of his. I was going to tell him after."

"I could totally understand why he thought it was you. I mean, come on. I never would have thought in a million years your mom would get pregnant again."

"You and me both."

As the confusion and sadness was swept away by the tide, an anger roared throughout my body. Getting up from the table, I walked over to the counter and downed a shot of tequila. Slamming my fists on the counter, I looked at Sienna.

"So he just ran away?" I yelled. "Like a fucking coward? Instead of asking me or talking to me about it, he took off?"

My voice raised so loudly that I was sure the whole building heard.

"Calm down there, tiger." She put her hands up. "But it looks that way."

"FUCK HIM!" I shouted as I threw the vase of daisies he gave me at the wall and it shattered all over the floor with water spilling everywhere.

"Okay. Seriously, Chloe, calm down. This isn't like you. Take a deep breath. Come on. Deep breath," she spoke as she breathed in and out.

Following her lead, I took in several deep breaths to try and calm myself. After about the fourth one, my heart started to settle down.

"That a girl." She walked over to me and wrapped her arms around me. "I'm sorry he sucks. You need to tell him that you aren't pregnant."

"I'm not telling him anything. If he thinks I'm pregnant, let him think it. It's over between us for good. He showed his true colors with this and it's something I don't think I'll ever be able to forgive him for."

"Come, let's sit down on the couch and be rational about this." She took hold of my arm and walked me to the couch.

"Are you defending him?" I narrowed my eyes at her.

"No. I'm not defending him at all. What he did was a total douchebag move. But aren't you the one who said that he was broken inside? You knew exactly what you were getting into when the two of you became a couple. This shouldn't shock you."

"But it does! He turned his back on his child and the mother of his child. A woman he supposedly loves."

She held up her finger. "Now remember, he never told you that he loved you. He just always said 'me too,' which, if you stop and think about it, he's actually saying he loves himself too."

"Ugh! You aren't helping!" I brought my knees up to my chest and wrapped my arms around my legs. "He grew up without a family. His parents abandoned him and now he did the same thing." A tear formed in my eye.

"Hold up. You're not even pregnant, so technically, he didn't abandon his child because a child does not exist."

"But to him it does. He thinks I'm pregnant, so he ABANDONED his child!" I yelled.

"Stop yelling at me, Chloe. Meditate, do something."

As I shook my head, the tears in my eyes began to fall down my face.

"I can't believe he would do something like this. I thought I knew him, but obviously I don't."

"Aw, sweetie," she whispered as she placed her hand on my arm. "You do know him and you know how he struggles with relationship things. I mean, he's trying so hard and now he thinks you're pregnant and he got scared. You know what babies men are."

"So you are defending him?"

"No. I'm just trying to make you see it from his point of view. He never had a family and now he has this amazing girlfriend who loves him to the ends of the earth and then here comes baby. Instant family. He's scared, Chloe."

"I guess you're right, but I DON'T GIVE A SHIT!"

"There you go with the yelling again."

"I'm done. I don't deserve this. I'm a good person, Sienna."

"Of course you are. You're the sweetest, most kind hearted, and giving person I know. But I still think you need to tell him you're not pregnant."

"No." I shook my head. "He can think it all he wants. I'm done with him. Finished."

"And what are you going to do when he gets back and wants to talk?"

"He doesn't get to talk. He lost that right the minute he walked out my door. If it's so easy for him to stay away from me for a week or so, then it'll be a fuck of a lot easier to stay away the rest of his life."

"Chloe, I'm worried. This doesn't even sound like you."

"I'm hurt, Sienna. Don't you understand that?"

She kissed the side of my head. "Of course I do. But you don't have a mean bone in your body. You never have."

"Maybe that's my problem. I've let too many guys walk all over me all these years. Not this time. He made his bed over an assumption and now he can rot in it."

She heavily sighed as she tried to comfort me. "I think you mean he can sleep in it."

"No. He can rot for all I care. In fact, where's my phone?" I stormed off the couch and into the kitchen.

"Chloe, what are you doing?" Sienna asked in a panicked voice.

When I dialed Sebastian's number, it went straight to voicemail.

"Sebastian, it's Chloe. I know why you left New York. I just had to tell you that. Because letting you know that I know in some weird way gives me a sense of peace. When you decide to come back, don't call me, come to my apartment, the art gallery, nothing. It's over between us. I will erase every memory we ever made and I will move on with my life. I suggest you do the same. And by the way, if you follow me again like you did last time, I will get a restraining order against you! Consider yourself warned."

"Jesus, Chloe. I can't believe you just did that," Sienna spoke as she stood across the room with her mouth hanging open.

"Sienna, I love you, but I need to be alone right now."

"Are you sure? I can stay the night."

"No." I gave her a gentle smile. "Go home to Sam and I'll call you tomorrow."

"Okay." She pouted as she walked over and gave me a tight hug. "If you need me, call."

As soon as she left, I locked the door, started the water for a bath, climbed in the tub, and cried myself into oblivion.

Chapter 34

Sebastian

I was sitting at the bar in the Terrence Lounge when I finally decided to listen to Chloe's message. My heart shattered into a million pieces hearing her say those words to me. I spent my mornings running along the water and my days sitting on a bench in Waterfront Park, thinking and watching couples walk by hand in hand, kissing and smiling. I paid even closer attention to those couples pushing their babies in strollers. I watched a father as he held his crying baby, trying to calm down his son. I spent my nights sitting at the same bar, drinking my worries and problems away. Being away from her was so hard. I missed her touch, the feel of her soft skin, and the way her nose wrinkled every time she laughed. But what I missed most was hearing her say that she loved me. And now I would never hear those words again because of what I'd done. I could tell by the tone in her voice that she hated me. She was hurt that I left and somehow she figured out why. Lies always do come back to bite you in the ass.

"Another bourbon, my friend?" the young bartender asked with a smile.

"Sure. Why not."

"You've been in here the past four nights. Are you from around here?"

"Nah. I'm from New York."

"Ah, I love New York. Bartended there for a couple of years."

"Oh yeah? Why did you move to Seattle?"

"My girlfriend is from here. We met in New York when she attended NYU. It was love at first sight. She found out she was pregnant right when she took a job here in Seattle. So I moved with her. We're getting married next month." He pulled his phone from his pocket. "This is my little angel, Christina."

"She's beautiful."

"She's my pride and joy. Her and her mother. Two best things that ever happened to me my whole life."

"Congratulations."

"Thanks, man. How about you? Do you have a family back home?"

"No." I shook my head. "In fact, my girlfriend just broke up with me over voicemail."

"Ouch. Sorry to hear that."

Just as he was about to walk away, his phone rang.

"Hey, baby. I was just talking about you. Okay, I'll pick some up on the way home. I love you too, baby. Tell my angel that Daddy will home in a couple of hours."

Finishing off my drink, I headed back to the hotel and climbed into bed. As I was scrolling through the pictures of us in Hawaii, I came across one that was more special than any others I had. The picture of Chloe sleeping that first night in London. I took it before I left that morning. She didn't know I took it and she still didn't know to this day. I traced my finger over her picture as if magically, she'd appear in bed next to me. I looked at that picture every night after London, wondering if I would have stayed if things would have been different. But now, she hated me and threatened to get a restraining order if I came near her. Nonetheless, she was pregnant with my child and that was the one thing she couldn't keep from me. I knew what I had to do and, in a couple of days, I would return home to claim what was mine.

****

Chloe

By time I dragged my sad, sorry ass out of bed, it was one o'clock. The only reason I did was because my parents decided to drop by.

"What's going on with you?" my mom asked with worry. "We ran into Sienna this morning and she asked if you had talked to us yet, but she wouldn't tell us anything else."

"You okay, pumpkin?" my dad asked.

I sighed as I went to the kitchen to make some tea.

"Sebastian thinks I'm the one who's pregnant. He found the test in the bathroom and flew out of here as fast as he could. He left town and I haven't heard from him since."

"Oh, sweetheart. Come here." My mom held out her arms.

I should have broken down and cried in her arms, but the truth was, I had cried so much the past couple of days that I didn't have any tears left in me.

"Why would he do something like that without talking to you?" my dad asked.

"Oh. I don't know. Maybe because he's an asshole."

"Now, Chloe. What have I taught you about calling people names?"

Rolling my eyes, I grabbed a couple of tea bags and put them in the teacups.

"Sounds to me like he's running scared," my dad spoke as he reached in the fridge for a beer. "I'll have a talk with him."

"No, Dad. I broke up with him."

"But you're not even pregnant," my mom said.

"I know that, but he thinks I am and instead of talking to me, he took the cowardly way out and left. I'm taking that as a sign for the future. The universe is telling me to run as fast as I can away from him."

"No. I don't believe that." My mom shook her head. "The two of you are meant to be together. That's why you found each other again when you moved back here."

"Well, he hurt me, again, and I'm not playing anymore. This game hurts me, Mom. It hurts so bad that I don't know how long it's going to take for me to fully recover because I loved him so much."

"You know what they say, absence makes the heart grow fonder," my dad chimed in. "Maybe he'll come back groveling on his hands and knees, begging you for forgiveness."

"I doubt it. I told him that if he ever came near me again, I'd file a restraining order against him."

"Oh, Chloe." My mom placed her hand on my face.

"Enough talk about Sebastian. It's over, so get used to it. We have other things to focus on, like my baby brother or sister." I smiled as I placed my hand on my mom's belly.

Monday morning had arrived and it was the start of a new week. I set my alarm earlier than usual so I could meditate before heading to work. It was a new day. A day where I would renew my soul and create a peaceful mind. A mind that was free from any thoughts of him. He would now become a distant memory of a love I once had. A man who made me feel like I was the only woman on the face of the earth but also a man who broke my heart in two. Just as I prepared myself to meditate, my phone rang and it was Sienna. When I answered it, she was brushing her teeth.

"Oh good. You're up. Sam brought up a good point last night." She paused to spit in the sink.

"It's a new day, Sienna. I don't want to hear any points. Now, if you'll excuse me, I'm getting ready to meditate before work."

"'Ello, Chloe." Sam appeared on the screen.

"Good morning, Sam." I sighed.

"Okay, so you know how you broke it off with Sebastian?"

"Yes."

"Well, he isn't going anywhere because he thinks you're carrying his child. So, he's going to be checking on you from time to time to see how you're doing."

"And you know this how, Sam?"

"Because I'm a guy, Chloe. We all think alike. You better prepare that pretty little head of yours because you ain't seen the last of him. The only way that's going to happen is if you tell him you're not pregnant."

So much for my renewed soul and peaceful mind.

"I have to go, Sam. Thanks for the little pep talk." I gave him a thumbs-up.

"No problem, love. Have a good day."

"Talk to you later, Chloe." Sienna waved in the background.

As I was unpacking some new paintings that arrived, I heard a familiar voice say my name.

"Chloe."

I stood as if I was frozen in time, unable to move. My heart began to rapidly beat and my palms started to sweat. Staring down at the large wooden carton, I spoke, "Go away, Sebastian. It's over."

"We need to talk."

"And we could have, but your time expired and now, you don't get to talk to me."

"You need to listen to what I have to say, Chloe."

I spun myself around out of anger and stared into the eyes of a man that I so deeply loved.

"You shouldn't have left. You should have talked to me that night when you saw the pregnancy test. You should have texted me back or at least called me. I would have explained everything to you. But you didn't. You shut me out of your life for a week. We were in a relationship. You don't do that to someone you care about." Tears filled my eyes.

"I was scared. I panicked and I needed to clear my head."

"And what about me? Didn't you think that I would be scared? That maybe I needed you more than ever? Did you ever once stop to think about someone other than yourself?"

Suddenly, Gregory walked upstairs. "Umm. Can you two keep it down? We have customers in the gallery."

"Sorry, Gregory."

I went into my office and Sebastian followed.

"I thought about you every second of every day. You are a permanent thought in my head. But, Chloe, the thought of having a baby scared the shit out of me. You know me and you know my past. I had to question whether or not I could even be a good father. I know nothing about kids. Hell, I've never even held a baby before and I'm terrified. I've already let you down several times and the thought of letting my kid down sent me over the edge."

"Well, guess what? I'm going to put your mind at ease. I'm not pregnant." I threw my hands out to the side.

"What? What do you mean you're not pregnant?"

"I'M. NOT. PREGNANT."

"So you lied to me?" he spoke with seriousness.

"Lied to you? How the fuck could I lie to you when I never told you that I was pregnant!" I shouted.

"But the test was in your garbage."

"Yes, because my mom is the one who's having a baby. Not me, you idiot. I couldn't wait to tell you that night, but you never gave me the chance to. From the minute you walked through the door, it was all about the deal you made, which was fine, but then you saw the test and ran out of my apartment like the coward you are. All of this could have been avoided. But you know what? I'm happy it happened this way because it was sign. A sign that we shouldn't have a future together."

"Chloe, you don't mean that."

"Just like you didn't mean to walk out on me, Sebastian, when you thought I was pregnant? Do you remember that day in the park when you told me that it could never work between us? Well, you were right."

I grabbed my phone and my purse and stormed out of my office.

"Chloe!" Sebastian shouted. "I love you."

I stopped for a brief moment, took in a deep breath, and walked down the stairs and out of the gallery. Hearing those words finally come from him should have made me happy but instead they cut into my heart like a sharp blade. I didn't care that he said it. I was so blinded by anger and hurt that I couldn't see or think straight. I was headed to God knows where as I hurried down the street, just wanting to get away from him for the fear if I stayed and listened to him any longer, I'd fall back into his arms.

After about thirty minutes, I headed back to the gallery. Stepping inside, I looked around and Gregory came walking up to me.

"Is he still here?" I asked.

"No. He left right after you did. What the hell is going on between you two?"

"Long story and I apologize for what happened. It'll never happen again."

Gregory hooked his arm around me and smiled. "No worries, Chloe."

Chapter 35

Sebastian

I wasn't taking no for an answer. She still loved me. I could see it in her eyes and now I needed to do everything in my power to try and get her back. Chloe Kane missing from my life wasn't an option. Now I was on a mission, but I'd give her a few days to settle down, clear her head, and then I'd make my move. We were meant to be together and that was exactly what we were going to be. While in Seattle, I made a self-discovery and finally realized my purpose in life. It wasn't to run a billion-dollar company. My purpose in life was to love Chloe and take care of her both physically and emotionally, and that was exactly what I planned to do. I finally felt free by accepting the overwhelming feelings I had for her. My fears of hurting her and letting her down dissipated. Some were still there, but once I focused on my true feelings and what really mattered, I had finally stopped being my own worst enemy.

Stopping at the florist before heading to the office, I ordered eight dozen gerbera daisies, all in beautiful glass vases to be delivered to her office tomorrow.

"Would you like to include a card?" the saleswoman asked.

"No." I gently smiled. "She'll know who they're from. I want them delivered one dozen every hour."

"That's really sweet. She's going to love it."

"I hope so." I winked as I walked out of the shop.

I should have felt down about what happened earlier, for the things she said and the hurt and sadness that resided in her eyes. But I didn't because I was going to take away her pain and sadness and give her a life of love and happiness. She deserved the world and I was the one who was going to make sure she got it. I wasn't worried about her rejecting me. She just needed time, like I did, and I would respect that and give her what she needed, even if it took days, weeks, months, or years. I wasn't going anywhere and when she was ready, she'd be back in my arms forever. Once I had her, I was never letting go.

Chapter 36

Chloe

After work, I had locked myself away in my apartment while I ate a pint of cookie dough ice cream and watched *The Notebook*. Tears streamed down my face, and suddenly, I became a blubbering mess. Being in the fragile emotional state I was in, maybe that wasn't the best choice of a movie to watch. I threw the ice cream carton away and headed to the bathroom to brush my teeth. Opening the drawer, I saw that his toothbrush still lay next to mine, as did his deodorant, shaver, shaving cream, and the stupid tube of Colgate toothpaste because he didn't like the kind I had.

"UGH!" I balled my fists.

I quickly made my way to the hall closet where I stored a couple of small boxes. Grabbing one, I threw all of his things from the bathroom in it. Walking over to my dresser and opening the drawer, I took out all the clothes he had kept here for when he spent the night. My mind was at full speed and I couldn't seem to control myself. Slipping on my slippers and throwing a light coat over my pajamas, I grabbed the box and hailed a cab to his penthouse. Upon entering the building, the doorman stopped me.

"Miss Kane, are you all right?"

"Just peachy, Jeffrey. Now if you'll excuse me, I have to give Mr. Bennett his things."

"Here, let me get the elevator for you."

"Thank you." I nodded.

Stepping off the elevator, I set the box down and began to walk away. I stopped halfway down the hall when the thought that someone might steal his things crossed my mind. Would I care? Yeah. I would, so I walked back, rang the doorbell, and quickly walked away. I wasn't fast enough when I heard the door open and Sebastian call my name.

"Chloe?"

Shit. Double shit.

I turned around and saw him standing there in his pajama bottoms and a tight fitting t-shirt. The way his shirt hugged his muscular body always got me.

"You brought my stuff back in your pajamas?"

"Yes! I wanted it out of my apartment."

"And you couldn't wait until morning, why?"

"Because. I wanted it out now."

The corners of his mouth curved upwards.

"Since you're here, I can give you your things."

"No. You can drop them off at my apartment when I'm not home. Preferably when I'm at work. In fact, you can just have Eli do it. Good night, Sebastian." I turned and walked away.

I heard him snicker. "Good night, Chloe." And then the door shut. Why the fuck was he snickering? Better yet, why was he smiling? When I reached the lobby, I gave Jeffrey a wave.

"Do you feel better now, Miss Kane?"

"Yes. Much better." I hailed a cab and headed home.

****

Sebastian

Shutting the door, I couldn't help but laugh. That was my girl. Some people would have found it strange that she came all the way here in her pajamas to drop off my things, but not me, I expected nothing less of her. That was one of the things I loved about Chloe; she was unpredictable and the most adorable girl I had ever known. I set the box down in the hallway. There was no way I was packing up her stuff because there was no need to. She'd be back and they'd be here waiting for her. If it made her feel better to drop my things off in the late hours of the night in her pajamas, then so be it. As long as she felt better, that was all that mattered.

****

Chloe

Stepping into the gallery at approximately eight fifty-five, I was running a little late because I decided to make a Starbucks run for all of us.

"Thank you, Chloe." Gregory and the rest of the crew smiled.

"Today's going to be a fantastic day." I grinned.

As I was walking up the stairs to my office, I heard, "I have a delivery for Chloe Kane."

Turning around, I saw a man standing there with a vase full of gerbera daisies.

Rolling my eyes, I asked Gregory to sign for them and bring them up. I knew who they were from. I could have easily told the delivery guy to take them back, but they were so pretty and would look so nice in my office. Just because they were from him, it didn't matter. I wasn't about to send perfectly good flowers away.

It was ten o'clock and as I was sitting at my desk, Gregory walked in.

"Another delivery for you." He smiled.

"Again?" I asked as I looked at the brightly colored red gerbera daisies.

"Where would you like them?"

"Just put them over there." I pointed towards the window.

This went on all day. At the start of each hour, a new bouquet was delivered. It was a little after four o'clock when Connor walked into my office.

"What the hell happened in here? Are you secretly running a florist?" He smiled.

I sighed. "Sebastian."

"Ah. I see. I take it that he's trying to make amends," Connor spoke as he sat down.

"He can try all he wants. It's not happening."

"If you don't mind my asking, what exactly did he do?"

"It's a long story, so I'll give you the shortened version. He thought I was pregnant and then he took off to Seattle and I didn't hear from him for days. He lied to me, he ignored my calls and texts, and now he thinks he can just waltz back into my life as if his leaving based on something that wasn't true was no big deal."

"Can I give you a little bit of advice?" He smiled.

"Sure. Why not?" I spoke in a sarcastic tone as I leaned back in my chair.

"Sometimes, we men get scared and make stupid decisions. Hell, I'll be the first to admit that I've done some really stupid things where Ellery was concerned. So stupid that it threatened our relationship more times that I care to recall."

"Really? But you two are so perfect."

"Thank you. We are perfect, aren't we?" He grinned. "But we weren't always perfect. We had our troubles along the way and we both made our share of huge mistakes. What I'm trying to say, Chloe, is that making mistakes is how relationships grow and it's what makes them stronger. If I had given up on Ellery or she had given up on me, we never would have made it to where we are today. Sometimes we have to step outside the box and take a look at the bigger picture. Once you do that, you'd probably see that more good can come from it than standing inside that little box. Does that make sense?"

Narrowing my eyes at him, I spoke, "Yeah. I think it does. So you're basically saying that it's okay for him to continuously hurt me and I should just take it." I smiled.

"God no. That's not what I'm saying at all. You love Sebastian and he loves you. I see it in his expression every time you two are together. People tend to do stupid things because they love the other person so much that it frightens them. But it's those things that strengthen the bond between two people, unless one of them cheated. Now that's a different story. You always see the good in people when everyone else only sees the bad. That's the first thing I noticed about you when you first came to work for me. In fact, I do believe you and Ellery were related in a past life."

"How did you get so wise?" I asked.

"By making tons of stupid mistakes in my relationship. Just ask Ellery." He sighed. "Actually, don't ask her because it would just make me look like a complete ass."

I couldn't help but laugh. "Thanks, Connor. I appreciate your advice."

He got up from his seat. "You're welcome. Oh. I stopped by to drop off a couple of Ellery's paintings. I left them down with Gregory."

"Great. I'll get them up before I leave."

"Enjoy the rest of your evening, Chloe." He winked.

"You too, Connor."

Chapter 37

Sebastian

It had been almost two weeks since I last saw Chloe. I still smiled when I thought about her standing in the hallway of my building in her pajamas. I respected her wishes and didn't try to contact her. I was still giving her time and we'd cross paths again when the time was right.

I had just finished a business lunch and was walking down the street back to the office, when my phone beeped with a text message from Damien. Quickly responding and looking down, I bumped shoulders with someone.

"I'm—Chloe." I spoke in shock.

"Sebastian."

"Hello, Sebastian." Ophelia smiled.

"Hello there, Ophelia. It's nice to see you again. By the way, congratulations."

"Why, thank you."

I couldn't take my eyes off Chloe. "Do you have the day off?" I asked her.

"I took a half day. We went crib shopping."

"Sounds fun. Well, I need to get back to the office. It was good seeing you, Chloe."

"Yeah. Good seeing you too, Sebastian."

Ophelia placed her hand on my arm before I walked away.

"You should come to my yoga class on Sunday. It starts at nine o'clock. I think you'd enjoy it. There are other men in the class, so you don't have feel embarrassed about being there. Many corporate men do yoga. Did you know that?"

"No. Actually, I didn't."

"It's a great stress reliever. Plus, it helps you to connect with your spiritual being. It clears your mind and opens the gate to better clarity. What happens when your mind is clear and your body is free of stress?"

"What?" I smiled.

"You're able to allow new ideas and better decision making to flow through."

"Maybe I will."

"Aw, that would be great. Wouldn't it, Chloe?"

"I don't know. I can't see you doing yoga." She looked at me.

"It never hurts to try new things. It was nice seeing you both, but I have to get back to the office."

When I stepped into my office, Damien was sitting behind my desk.

"Hey. Have you ever taken a yoga class?"

"A couple of times. Why?"

"I was just wondering. Someone told me that a lot of corporate men take it."

"Are you thinking about taking one?" he asked.

"I don't know."

"Does this have anything to do with Chloe?"

"No."

"Liar!" He laughed as he got up from my chair. "Do what you have to do to prove to her that you still love her and want her back. If that means taking a yoga class, then do it."

It was Sunday morning, and while I showered, I tried to think about what to wear to yoga class. I couldn't believe I was actually going, but I was doing it for Chloe. Okay, I was doing it for me too. Being able to see her, even if it was only for an hour, was better than not seeing her at all, no matter what the circumstances were. I had no clue what to wear as I stared inside all my opened drawers. Grabbing my phone from the nightstand, I decided to suck it up and send a quick text message to Chloe. I highly doubted she would respond, but it was worth a try.

"Good morning. I'm sorry to bother you but I have a quick question. What does one wear to a yoga class?"

"LOL. You're actually coming?"

"Yes. I could use some mental clarity at the moment."

"Wear your black athletic pants that are in the second drawer to the left and the matching black t-shirt that is hanging in your closet towards the back by your casual pants."

"Thank you."

"You're welcome."

Her "LOL" made me smile. The fact that she could laugh about me coming to her mother's yoga class told me that maybe, just maybe, the hate she had for me was starting to disappear. I couldn't wait to see her. When I wasn't up all night thinking about her, I was dreaming about her.

****

Chloe

What was he up to? He would be the last person on this earth that I ever expected to see at a yoga class. Just as I was about to walk out the door, my phone rang, and it was Sienna. When I answered it, I narrowed my eyes at her.

"Why are you still in bed? We have yoga in ten minutes."

"I can't make it today. I'm sorry." She pouted. "Me and Sam did our own yoga last night and now I can't seem to get out of bed."

"Me either," Sam mumbled.

I sighed. "I packed the picnic basket." I held it up.

"Please forgive me. I promise I'll make it up to you."

"Yeah. We'll make it up to you," Sam mumbled.

"Go back to bed. I'll call you later."

"Love you, buttercup."

"Love you, beautiful friend."

"Love you both too." I sighed.

When I arrived at the center, I looked around for Sebastian and didn't see him. Setting my mat down on the floor, I heard his voice next to me.

"Do you mind if I do yoga here?" He smiled.

Ugh. Why the fuck did he have to look so sexy? His black athletic pants and the black t-shirt that clung to his body sent shivers down my spine.

"No. Feel free. There's a mat over there."

"Ah. I guess I would need one of those."

I let out a soft giggle as he walked over and grabbed a mat. This was going to be good. Once class was over, I looked over and Sebastian was lying down on the mat.

"Class is over," I spoke. "You can get up now."

"Actually, I can't seem to move."

Laughing, I held out my hand. He moaned as he got up from the mat.

"That is a lot harder than it looks."

"It can be challenging." I smiled.

"So what did you think, Sebastian?"

"I feel very stress relieved, Ophelia."

"Good. I'm glad to hear that." She grinned.

"Well, I'm going to take off, Mom," I spoke as I gave her a kiss on the cheek. "I'll call you later. Bye, little sibling." I placed my hand on her growing belly.

"Bye, sweetheart. Thanks for coming, Sebastian."

"Thank you for suggesting it."

I grabbed the picnic basket I had sitting on the shelf in the back of the room.

"Going on a picnic?" Sebastian asked as he pointed to the basket.

"Yeah. Sienna was supposed to be here and then the two of us were going to have a girls' day at the park, but she had to cancel."

"Why?" he asked as he held the door open for me.

"Apparently, she and Sam did their own yoga last night and now neither one of them can get out of bed."

Sebastian chuckled. "I can understand that. I think. I'm going this way." He pointed to the right as I headed left. "Have a nice day and enjoy your picnic."

"Thanks." I gave a small smile.

What the hell was I doing? *Get it out of your head, Chloe.*

"Hey, Sebastian?"

He stopped walking and turned around. "Yeah?"

"You wouldn't by any chance want to come with me, would you? I mean, I packed all this food and I would hate to let it go to waste, considering there are so many starving people in this world."

"Are you sure?" He tucked his hands into his pockets.

"Yeah. I'm sure."

"I would love to join you." He smiled.

"Then let's go. We can walk since it's such a beautiful day."

We walked to Central Park and set up on the Great Lawn. Sebastian helped me spread out the blanket and then we took off our shoes and made ourselves comfortable.

"It's a beautiful day," I spoke as I took in the sun that was beating down on me.

"It sure is. We're not going to have too many days like this left."

"I know. Before you know it, Mother Nature will blow in the snow, cold, and ice."

Being here with him reminded me of times not too long ago. It felt weird because, as well as I knew him, and after all the things we had done together, it felt like we were two strangers sitting next to each other. I took to heart the conversation that Connor and I had a couple of weeks ago. Sebastian hadn't tried to contact me at all and I had wondered if he'd moved on with his life. It was gnawing at me, so I had to ask.

"So what have you been doing since you got back from Seattle?"

"Mainly working."

"Sounds boring." I smiled as I opened the picnic basket and took out the sandwiches and fruit.

"What have you been up to?"

"Not much. Just work, dinner with my parents, and an occasional night with Sienna and Sam."

"Sounds fun. Your mom is really starting to show."

"I know." I took a bite of my sandwich.

"I really can't believe she's pregnant. How old is she again?"

"Forty-six. It's going to be weird to have a little brother or sister who is twenty-five years younger than me."

"I bet. Just think, when he or she is twenty-five, you'll be the big five-o."

"Weird." I slowly shook my head and he laughed.

We continued our conversation, both of us treading carefully as not to bring up the subject of us. After a couple of hours, I found myself not wanting to leave him.

Chapter 38

Sebastian

Having a picnic with her in Central Park on such a beautiful day was more than I could ask for. I had missed her so much and being with her, even though we were no longer together, made me fall in love with her even more. It took every bit of control I had in me not to grab her mouth and kiss her beautiful soft lips. It was difficult for me because I wanted to touch her so badly. I wanted to wrap my arms around her and tell her that we could be us again, but I knew she wasn't ready.

"Thank you for the sandwiches and fruit." I gave her a smile.

"You're welcome. Thank you for joining me."

"My pleasure. I'm just sorry Sienna bailed on you. By the way, how long is Sam staying?"

"I guess forever." She laughed. "He applied for permanent residency in the U.S."

"That's good, right?"

"Sienna seems to really love him and he loves her. So, it's good."

"What about his family?"

"When his mom and dad divorced a few years back, his mom moved to Germany and his dad moved to Scotland with the woman he was cheating on his mom with."

"And his job?"

"Up and quit. He's going to find work here, eventually."

Looking in the picnic basket, I saw she had quite a bit of food left over.

"You sure packed a lot for just you and Sienna."

"Yeah. I packed a few extra things because on my way home, I'm going to stop and give the rest to Willie and his friends."

The corners of my mouth curved upwards as I stared into her eyes.

"That's a good idea. I'm sure they would be very grateful. Would you mind if I came with you?"

"Not at all. By the way, Willie told me that a guy named Sebastian has been stopping by and giving him a few dollars here and there."

I shrugged. "It's the least I can do to help him out. You know, I have never forgotten about what it was like for me living in that abandoned house. When I said to you that night that his being homeless was his own fault, I said it out of anger because it reminded me of bad times. All these years, I wouldn't even look at the homeless people on the street because every time I did, I went back to that time. A time I want to erase from my memory."

"You shouldn't want to erase those memories, Sebastian. That period of time in your life made you who are today. You should embrace it and maybe tell your story to others and inspire them. What you did was amazing and all it took was one person to put you on the right path. People come into our lives for a reason and they leave our lives for a reason. They only may be here temporarily, but they're there for a purpose."

I wanted to reach out and stroke her beautiful blonde hair and tell her that I knew the reason why she came into my life, but I couldn't. I didn't want to rock the boat, so to speak. I wanted to tell her that if she still was dating Corey when she went to London, we never would have met because the thought of having sex with a stranger in a foreign country never would have entered her mind.

"Do you think if we didn't see each other in London, we would have eventually met here in New York?"

She looked down. I could tell my question made her uncomfortable.

"I'm not sure. Why don't we go and give this food to Willie and the gang?"

"Sure. I'll call Eli and have him pick us up. It's a pretty long walk."

"It's a beautiful day, though, and the walk is good for us. Besides, if you don't keep moving, your muscles will tighten up from today, and you won't be able to get out of bed tomorrow."

I sighed. "Okay. If you insist."

We got up from the ground. While she folded the blanket, I grabbed hold of the picnic basket and we walked to where Willie was camping out for the day.

"Hey, Willie," Chloe spoke as she found him asleep, covered in a blanket on the cement in the alley.

He moaned and then coughed as he tried to open his eyes.

"Willie, are you okay?" I asked as I knelt down beside him.

Chloe placed her hand on his forehead. "He's burning up."

Pulling my phone out of my pocket, I spoke, "I'll call 911. He needs to see a doctor."

"It's okay, Willie, we're going to get you some help," she spoke.

The ambulance arrived and Eli pulled up behind.

"I'm going to ride with him in the ambulance," Chloe said.

"Okay. I'll meet you at the hospital."

"You don't have to, Sebastian. I'm sure you have other things to do."

Grabbing hold of her hand, I spoke, "I don't, and I want to."

A small smile crossed her lips as she gave me a nod and climbed into the back of the ambulance.

****

Chloe

As I was holding Willie's hand, his eyes opened while the paramedics gave him an I.V.

"You're going to be okay, Willie." I smiled.

"I don't think this time, kiddo."

"Don't say that. The doctors are going to make you feel better."

Once we arrived at the hospital, Sebastian wasn't too far behind as I was told to wait in the waiting room while the doctor examined him. I sat in the chair of the waiting room that contained a young girl and her screaming baby. Sebastian took a seat next to me and handed me a cup of coffee.

"I thought you could use this."

"Thanks." I took the cup from him.

"Someone over there isn't happy." He smiled.

"Are you talking about the baby or the mother?"

"Both. How old do you think she is?"

"She looks to be about seventeen or eighteen. Here, hold this." I handed him the cup and walked over to where the girl, who looked like she was going to lose it any second, sat. "Someone isn't very happy."

"No. She doesn't feel well and she won't stop crying. If she'd only stop for a minute, that would be great."

"May I?" I held out my arms to her.

The girl gave me a funny look and then looked over at Sebastian. "Do you think you can get her to stop?"

"I can give it a try." I smiled. "What's her name?"

"Isabelle. She's four months old," she spoke as she handed her baby over to me.

I walked around the waiting room with her and began singing *Tomorrow Is a Long Time* in her ear as I held her up to my shoulder and softly rubbed her small back. After a few choruses, she began to quiet down and fell asleep. Walking her back over to her mom, I carefully handed Isabelle to her.

"How did you do that?" she asked.

"Babies can sense when you're stressed out, which stresses them out. A little singing always works wonders."

"Thank you so much. Thank you." Tears filled her eyes.

"You're welcome. Unfortunately, when they call you back, she'll wake up again."

"That's fine. Just a few moments of quiet is all I need right now."

I gave her a small smile and went and sat down next to Sebastian.

"You're going to make a damn good mother one day." He smiled.

"Thanks." I took my coffee from him.

"And a damn good big sister."

"I'm really excited for the baby. It will be challenging for my parents since they haven't raised a kid in a number of years."

"You'll be there to help them out." He ran his hand down the back of my hair.

"You know, you don't have to stay," I spoke.

"Chloe, I'm here for both of you and I'm staying."

A doctor walked into the waiting room, asking who was with Willie. Sebastian and I stood up.

"We are," I spoke.

"Willie has pneumonia and a pretty bad case of it. It seems he's had it for a while. Because his lungs were inflamed for a period of time, his oxygen levels dropped, which caused kidney damage. Not only that, but the bacteria spread into his bloodstream, and from what we can tell, has infected his heart. It's a good thing you got him in here when you did."

"Is he going to be okay, doctor?" Sebastian asked.

"We aren't sure." He looked down. "We're pumping him full of antibiotics right now, but only time will tell."

As the doctor was standing there talking to us, someone came on the overhead speaker.

"Code blue, room 104. Code blue, room 104."

"That's his room," the doctor spoke as he turned and ran down the hallway.

Sebastian and I ran behind him and watched through the window as they used the defibrillator and then CPR. Sebastian wrapped his arm around me and pulled me close.

"Time of death, three forty-five," the doctor spoke as he looked at the clock on the wall.

"No." Tears started to stream down my face as I buried my head in Sebastian's chest.

"I'm so sorry, baby." He tightened his arm around me as his other arm wrapped around me and softly rubbed my back.

The doctor walked out of the room and looked at us. "I'm sorry. We did everything we could."

"Can we go in there and say goodbye?" I asked.

"Yes," he spoke as he walked away.

While Sebastian held me, we walked into the room.

"Hey, Willie." I placed my hand on his. "You're home now and you won't have to suffer anymore. You'll always be warm and you'll never be hungry. Pretty cool, huh?"

Out of the corner of my eye, I saw Sebastian bring his hand up to his face. Oh my God, he was wiping away a tear. I didn't want to embarrass him or make a big deal of it, so I ignored it. My heart, which was full of sadness over Willie, was also full of happiness that Sebastian was finally able to shed a tear.

"Well, I think funeral arrangements need to be made," Sebastian spoke as he cleared his throat. "We're going to give him a proper burial, no expense spared."

"Really? You're going to do that for him?" I asked as I looked into his sad eyes.

"Of course. He wasn't only your friend, Chloe."

"Right." I gave a small smile. "Shall we head to the funeral home and make the arrangements now?"

"Let me call them first and make sure they can accommodate us today."

Sebastian stepped out into the hallway. Looking back to Willie, I spoke, "Hear that? Sebastian is giving you an all-expenses-paid funeral. Even though I don't believe in them, I'm going to let him do it anyway. It'll make him feel better."

"The funeral home said they can see us today. I told them we'd be over soon. That's if you're ready."

"I am."

As we walked out of the room, one of the nurses called out to us.

"Here's his bag that was brought in with him. Since you're his family, you should take it."

"Thanks." I gave a small smile.

Chapter 39

Sebastian

A tear fell from my eye today. The first tear I've had since I was five years old. Was the tear for Willie? Or was it for seeing Chloe so upset? I really didn't know, and at this point, it didn't matter. She needed me and I needed her.

In the room where the caskets were lined up, we walked around and looked at them. I came across a beautiful mahogany one with brass trim.

"This one is nice for him," I spoke as I stood in front of it.

"Yeah. It's nice," Chloe responded.

"You don't sound enthused about it."

"No. No. I am. It's nice," she hesitantly spoke. "If you like it, we should get it."

"Do you see one you like better?" I arched my brow at her.

"No. This one is fine."

"Chloe, are you okay? I get the feeling you don't want to do this."

"Is it that obvious?" I bit down on my bottom lip.

"Just a bit. I can take care of everything. I don't want you any more upset."

"It's not that this really upsets me, it's just not necessary."

"What's not necessary?" I asked.

"A casket that costs ten thousand dollars. We can lay his body in something a little cheaper."

"Oh. I was just trying to give him the best."

"I know you were." I smiled. "But it doesn't matter. His spirit is on the other side now and he's at peace. He doesn't care about a ten-thousand-dollar fancy casket. We can bury him in this one right here."

"But it's so plain." I frowned.

"So? It's going in the ground, Sebastian."

"Fine. If that's the one you want, I'll buy it. But, just for the record, I want to be buried in the ten-thousand-dollar casket."

"Of course you do." She smirked as she placed her hand on my chest.

After picking the casket, I had the funeral home make the arrangements at the cemetery.

"Just call me when you get the details sorted out," I spoke to the funeral director.

"Remember, just a burial. Quick and simple," Chloe spoke.

"Yes, ma'am. Quick and simple." The director turned his eyes to me.

I shrugged as we walked out.

****

Chloe

Sebastian came with me to tell Willie's friends about his death. They took it really hard and some even shed a few tears. I promised that we'd let them know exactly when the funeral was so if they wanted to attend, they could.

"I'd feel better if you'd let me walk you home," Sebastian said.

The truth was I didn't want to be alone and he was the person I wanted to be with. Spending the day with him meant more to me than anything and I was happy that he was with me when Willie passed away. To be honest, if he wasn't, I would have probably called him.

"I'd like that."

"Are you hungry?" he asked. "We could stop on the way and grab a pizza or something."

"Pizza sounds good."

After getting the pizza, we stepped into my apartment, sat down, and ate. The last time he had been here was when he bolted out the door. That seemed like forever ago, but in reality, it wasn't. It amazed me how time slowed when you were suffering from a broken heart.

"Are you going to go through Willie's bag?" he asked as he took a bite of his pizza.

"Yeah. We can do that after we eat."

"Don't you want to call your parents or Sienna and tell them what happened?"

"I will later. Right now, I just want to sit here and enjoy this pizza with you."

The corners of his mouth curved up into a captivating smile. My body was aching for him and his sensual touch. Sex with him was addicting. Even when I was so mad at him, my body still thought about all the things he'd done to it.

"Do you want to have sex?" I blurted out.

"Huh?" He nearly dropped his pizza.

I laughed. "Answer the question. Do you want to have sex with me?"

"Umm. Of course I do. It's all I fucking dream about."

I got up from my chair and climbed on his lap, straddling him and placing my hands on each side of his face.

"I've missed you and your cock." I grinned.

"And I've missed you and your pussy." He brought his lips to mine. "Is this real, Chloe?"

"As real as it gets, babe."

Our lips locked lightly at first, then our kiss became passionate. So passionate that it was making up for all the time we lost.

"God, I've missed you so much," he whispered.

"I've missed you too."

As our lips were still locked in a passionate kiss, I climbed off his lap and he got up from the chair. Breaking apart, I pulled my tank top over my head and quickly removed my bra, tossing it on the table. Swooping me up in his arms, he carried me to the bedroom and lay me down on the bed while he hovered over me and his mouth devoured mine. Breaking our kiss, he stood up and pulled off my tennis shoes and socks. Reaching for my pants, his hands pulled them down along with my panties and he tossed them on the floor. With a low growl, he stared at me as he quickly stripped out of his clothes and then grabbed my legs, pulling my ass towards the edge of the bed. He knelt down with my legs over his shoulders, and his tongue licked up my inner thigh, sending erotic spasms throughout. His lips lightly pressed against my aching spot while his tongue traced tiny circles around me. Holy shit. Once again, I was in heaven. I moaned and threw my head back in ecstasy while raising my hips for him to go deeper.

"Is this what you've been craving?" he moaned.

"Yes. Oh God, yes!" I belted out.

He looked up at me and smiled. A smile itself that could throw me straight into an orgasm.

****

Sebastian

She tasted sweet. Just like I remembered. I'd been waiting for this day for what seemed like forever. I already knew it would be worth the wait. I wanted nothing more but to pleasure her all night long; to take away her sadness, if only for a day. I wanted to make her feel loved and wanted, but most of all, I wanted to show her that she was the most beautiful and most important woman in the world. Nothing mattered to me anymore. Not my business, my money, nothing. Only her. She was the only thing in my life I needed and wanted.

Her moans became feral as I continued to devour her. My tongue circled around her swollen spot as my finger dipped inside her. The wetness that emerged from her excited me, and my cock was throbbing to be inside. But first things first. The noises that escaped her escalated as my fingers explored her.

"Uh. Uh," she cried out in pleasure.

"Come for me, baby," I spoke with bated breath.

"Oh God, Sebastian."

She arched her back and her legs tightened against me as she gave me the pleasure of tasting her sweet orgasm. She arched her back and propped herself up on her elbows, displaying her beautiful and perky breasts. Climbing on the bed, I dipped down and wrapped my lips around her hard nipple, sucking and nipping until the moans that escaped her satisfied me. Her hands roamed through my hair and then down my backside until they reached my ass with a firm grip.

"I need you inside me right now," she spoke, panting intensely.

"How bad?"

"Really bad. Please. You need to fuck me with everything you have."

Jesus, hearing her say those words sent me into overdrive as I crammed myself inside her with such force, we both gasped for air. Her legs wrapped around my waist as I pounded into her as hard as I could. Her pussy greeted me with warmth and I found myself lost in her. I needed to slow down because I wanted to make this last.

Hovering over her and slowing my movements, I stared into her eyes. This moment. The moment we reconnected with each other was immeasurable.

"I love you," I spoke in a low voice.

Her lips gave way to a smile as she placed her hand on my cheek.

"I love you too."

Chapter 40

Chloe

"I'm paralyzed again," Sebastian smiled as he tried to roll off of me.

"That's a good thing. Job well done, Mr. Bennett." I grinned.

With a moan, he rolled onto his back.

"Does this mean you aren't going to do yoga anymore?"

"Probably not."

"I didn't think so." I smiled.

Climbing from the bed, I slipped on my silk robe.

"Where are you going?" he asked.

"To go through Willie's bag. Maybe there's something in there we can bury with him."

"Hold on. Let me grab a pair of sweatpants. Oh, that's right. Someone dropped off all my stuff in her pajamas." He propped himself up on his elbows.

Damn. Staring at him on the bed like that totally naked had me raring to go again.

"Oh yeah. I did do that. Didn't I?" I picked up his underwear off the floor and threw them at him. "You have these." I smiled brightly.

"As soon as we're done going through Willie's bag, we'll go back to my place, where you already have clothes and stuff waiting for you."

"Are you inviting me to a sleepover, Sebastian?"

"Damn right I am. We're never spending another night apart."

With a smile, I walked over to the bed and climbed on top of him.

"Promise?" I brushed my lips against his.

"You have my word, baby."

Wrapping his arms tightly around me, he pulled me down on top of him.

"I'm never letting you go. No matter what happens, you're my girl forever."

"Forever is a long time."

"Time is all we have and I'm going to spend every moment of it with you. You are the priority in my life, Chloe, and I'm going to make you a very happy woman."

"You already have." Our lips tangled once more, which led to another round of fantastic sex.

I set my phone down on the table while I took a bottle of open wine from the refrigerator. It started to ring and Sebastian told me it was Sienna.

"Answer it for me," I spoke as I reached up into the cupboard and grabbed a couple of wine glasses.

"Oh, hello there, Sebastian," Sienna spoke. "So you're half naked, I see. Does someone want to tell me what the hell is going on?!" she voiced rather loudly.

Sebastian laughed as he handed me my phone.

"Chloe, sweetheart, what happened from the time I talked to you this morning? How did *he* happen?"

"Long story and I'll tell you tomorrow. I was going to call you. Willie passed away today."

"Oh no. I'm so sorry. Are you okay?"

"I'm sad, but he's in a better place now. I'm really going to miss him."

"I would offer to come over and comfort you, but I see some cock, I mean, someone already has."

"I heard that, Sienna, and yes, my big cock has already comforted her twice." He smiled.

"Care to show me how big it really is?" She smirked.

"Okay, you two. You've had your fun. I'll call you tomorrow."

"Blah. You're no fun, Chloe."

Sebastian opened Willie's bag and began taking out some of his things. At the bottom, he pulled out a small envelope with my name on it.

"This has your name on it," Sebastian spoke.

Taking the envelope from his hand, I opened it and inside was a key to a safety deposit box with a note that contained the name of the bank and the box number.

"That's strange. Why would a homeless man have a safety deposit box?" Sebastian asked.

"I don't know. Maybe he kept some personal things in it after he lost his house."

"I'll come pick you up at the gallery tomorrow during lunch and we'll go check it out."

"Okay." I smiled.

"Are you ready to head to my penthouse?"

"Yes. Just let me grab a few things because I have a feeling I won't be back here for a while."

"Good idea. You may be held hostage."

"Mhmm. Are you going to tie me up and have your way with me?"

Sebastian closed his eyes for a second and took in a sharp breath.

"Chloe, don't say things like that or we'll never make it back to my place."

I giggled as I went into the bedroom and packed a few things. As Sebastian took my bag from me, I went into the kitchen.

"What are you getting now?" he asked.

I reached into the refrigerator and grabbed the two cans of whipped cream I had sitting in the door.

"Just these." I smiled.

"For what?"

"Really, Sebastian?" I placed my hand on my hip.

"Oh." His eyes lit up. "Damn it, Chloe. My cock is getting hard and we have to go."

I giggled as I walked out the door and Sebastian followed behind. Climbing into the limo, I said hi to Eli.

"It's nice to see you again, Chloe." He smiled.

"Nice to see you too, Eli. I brought the whipped cream." I winked as I held up the cans. "Can't have sex without it."

I looked over at Sebastian as he took in a deep breath.

"Really? Did you really have to tell him that?"

****

Looking at the clock, I saw it was almost lunchtime and Sebastian would be here soon to pick me up. Getting up from my desk, I walked downstairs as he was walking through the door.

"Ready, baby?" He smiled.

"Yes. Gregory, I'll be back in about an hour."

"You two enjoy your lunch." He smiled.

As we entered the bank, Seymour Rawlings, the bank manager, and according to Sebastian, number one ass kisser, walked up to us.

"Good day, Mr. Bennett. I didn't know you were stopping by the bank today. May I offer you and the beautiful lady some champagne?"

"Oh. You have champagne?" I asked with a grin.

"No. We're fine. Thank you, Seymour."

"We want champagne, Seymour." I patted his shoulder.

"Very good. Now, what brings you into our bank today?"

"I need to use my safety deposit box," I spoke as I held up the key.

"Oh. Yes. Please follow me."

We followed him to the room where the boxes were stored. Taking the key from my hand, he unlocked it and pulled the box out and set it on the long table in the middle of the room.

"There you go, Miss...?"

"Chloe. You can call me Chloe."

"Nice to meet you. And you're a friend of Mr. Bennett's?"

"Oh yes. We're lovers." I grinned.

Sebastian threw his head back and slowly shook it.

"Ah, excellent. Your champagne will be in shortly." He walked out of the room.

"Why did you tell him that?" Sebastian asked.

"Why not? Do you not want people knowing?"

"Of course I want people to know, but you could have said that I was your boyfriend. You didn't have say 'lover' in the seductive way you did."

I shrugged. "Obviously, I'll get some free perks being your lover, so why not?" I smiled.

He chuckled. "Open the box. Let's see what Willie, the homeless man, stored in here."

I slowly lifted the lid to the box, which stored his Medal of Honor.

"Oh look. We can bury this with him," I spoke.

"Umm. There's an envelope with your name on it."

Picking up the thick white envelope, I gasped when I opened it.

"Holy shit, Sebastian. Look at all this money!"

"Give me that." He took it from my hand and removed the money that sat inside. "What the fuck? How did he have all this?" Pulling out a folded piece of paper, he handed it to me. It was a letter from Willie.

"Dearest, Chloe,

If you're reading this, that means I've finally crossed over to the other side. You were the only non-homeless person who cared about me. It was pretty lonely when you moved out to California, except when your mom and dad would come to visit. The highlight of my life was the first day you moved back and I saw you walking down the street towards me. I don't want you to think I never listened to what you told me, because I did. To me, living on the streets had become a way of life I didn't mind. I have over fifty thousand dollars in the box that I hid away before I lost everything else. The money is yours. It's my way of thanking you for being such a wonderful human being and my best friend. I've never told you this, but you were like a daughter to me. I know you're not a materialistic person, so do whatever you would like with the money. Maybe open up your own gallery or buy some great art with it so you'll always remember me. Another thing, at the bottom of the box, there's the names of my children listed on a piece of paper with their last known address. Please just let them know that I've passed on. They have the right to know, even if they don't care. Take care, Chloe, and I hope you get everything you want out of life, although I have no doubt you will. Tell the gang I'll always be watching over them. Love, Willie."

Tears streamed down my face as I read his letter.

"Are you okay?" Sebastian asked.

Wiping the tears from my eyes, I spoke, "Yeah."

"I can't believe he had all this money and never spent it. His life could have been so different," Sebastian spoke.

"The money wasn't important to him. He liked the way he lived his life."

Seymour walked in with two glasses of champagne and a plate of chocolate truffles.

"Is everything okay?" he asked with concern.

"We just had a friend who passed away," I replied.

"Oh dear, I'm so sorry for your loss. If there's anything I can do, please let me know."

"Thank you, Seymour," Sebastian spoke.

Taking the contents of the box, Sebastian and I stepped outside of the bank.

"Do you want to grab something to eat?" he asked.

"Sure. But can we eat it somewhere special?"

"Of course, anywhere you want." He smiled as his lips brushed against mine.

Stopping at a deli near my apartment, we took our sandwiches over to the spot where Willie sat every day.

"What are you doing?" Sebastian asked as I sat down on the cement and leaned my back up against the brick wall.

"Eating lunch. Sit." I patted the cement.

"I'm wearing a three-thousand-dollar suit, Chloe."

"And?"

"And you want me to sit on the cement and eat a sandwich."

"And?" I cocked my head with a serious look.

"And, I guess this is as good a spot as any," he spoke as he sat down next to me.

Chapter 41

Chloe

Five Months Later

"This is the last box, Mr. Bennett," the muscularly built Channing Tatum lookalike moving man spoke.

"Thank you." Sebastian reached into his pocket and pulled out some cash. "You're all moved in now and you're never leaving." He smiled as he wrapped his arms around me.

"I'll agree to that." I kissed his lips.

"Now, let's go break in the bed."

"We've already broken it in thousands of times." I laughed.

"Not as an official living together couple we haven't."

"Ah. Let's go then, tiger." I pulled him by his tie to the bedroom.

Just as Sebastian thrust into me, my phone rang.

"Who is it?" I asked with bated breath as his thrusts were hard and deep.

"Really, Chloe?"

"Just look over at the nightstand. It could be my parents."

He looked over at my phone as he moved in and out of me.

"It's your dad. He can wait until we're finished."

"Give me the phone. It could be important. You know the baby is due."

Sebastian sighed, pulled out of me, and handed me my phone.

"Hey, Dad. What's up?" I put him on speaker.

"Hi, pumpkin. I'm not interrupting anything, am I?"

"We were in the middle of having sex, but it's okay."

Sebastian tilted his head and shot me a look.

"Sorry, Sebastian," my dad spoke.

"It's fine, Larry."

"We're at the hospital. Your mom is in labor."

"Eek! We're on our way."

"It could take hours, pumpkin. Go ahead and finish having sex. We'll be here when you're done."

"Thanks, Dad. We'll see you soon. Tell Mom I love her."

"Will do."

"The baby's coming." I grinned as I pulled him on top of me. "Now, where were we?"

Sebastian sat up and looked down at his cock.

"You and your dad ruined it, baby. How can I stay hard when you told your father we were having sex? Why do you have to always tell them?"

"Aw, they love that we have so much sex. You should be used to that by now."

"I'm not sure I'll ever get used it." He smiled. "Come on, let's get dressed and head to the hospital."

"Okay." I flew off the bed.

****

As Sebastian and I entered my mom's room, I ran over and grabbed her hand.

"The baby is coming," I said with excitement.

"You don't have to tell me twice," my mom spoke in irritation as she let out a howl.

"Just breathe through it, Mom." I held her hand.

Looking over at Sebastian, I could tell he was beginning to sweat.

"Are you okay?" I asked.

"I'm just going to wait out in the waiting room. Hang in there, Ophelia." He held up his fist as he walked out of the room.

When I rolled my eyes, my mom squeezed my hand.

"Go out there with him, sweetheart. He needs you. Your dad will let you know as soon as the baby's born."

"Are you sure, Mom?"

"Of course. I'm fine. But Sebastian, he didn't look so good." She smiled.

I kissed her forehead and walked to the waiting room.

"Hey, are you okay?" I asked as I stroked his arm.

"I'm fine. It's just seeing your mom in so much pain made me a little nervous."

"Aw, but the end result is worth the pain." I smiled.

He leaned over and kissed me just as Sienna and Sam walked in.

"Oh my God! Our baby is about to be born!" she exclaimed as she ran over and hugged me.

"I know. It should be any time now."

The four of us sat there patiently. Sebastian and Sam chatted it up while Sienna and I looked up makeup tutorials on our phones. Four hours later, my dad walked into the room.

"It's a boy!" he shouted. "I have a son!"

With a smile, I got up from my seat and gave him a hug. "And I have a brother. How's Mom?"

"She's great. Wait until you see him, Chloe. He's beautiful."

"When can we see them?"

"In a few minutes. I'll be right back to get you."

Sebastian walked over and wrapped his arms around me.

"Congratulations, big sister."

"Thank you. Let's go down to the gift shop and get some of those 'It's A Boy' balloons."

After purchasing six balloons, it was time to meet my brother. Walking into the room, a tear sprang to my eye when I saw my mom holding him in her arms.

"Mom. He's so beautiful." I kissed his tiny head.

"Chloe, I would like you to meet your brother, Arlo Benjamin Kane."

"Arlo. Wow. What a cool name." I smiled as she handed him to me.

****

Sebastian

I nearly lost my breath as I watched Chloe holding her brother. Things were so good between us. Actually, they were great. Greater than I ever could have imagined. These past five months, and spending every moment with her, made me view life in a whole new way.

"Come here." She smiled as she looked at me. "Come meet my brother."

Walking over to her, I stared down at the little guy as he quietly slept.

"Wanna hold him?" she asked.

"No. That's okay. He's too tiny."

"He won't break. Hold out your arms."

"Seriously, Chloe. He's sleeping. I don't want to disturb him."

"Pfft, you won't disturb him. This little guy had a long journey down the birth canal. Trust me, he's exhausted. Now, hold out your arms," she spoke in a soft voice.

This made me nervous. I had never held a baby before. As I held out my arms, Chloe gently handed him over.

"Hold his head," she spoke.

I smiled as I looked down at him. He definitely was beautiful and I saw a lot of Chloe in him. Especially his cute little nose.

"See, it's not so bad. Is it?" she asked.

I glanced up at her as a small smile crossed my lips. After spending some time with her parents, the baby, Sienna, and Sam, we said our goodbyes and headed home. As I climbed into bed, Chloe walked out of the bathroom with a toothbrush in her mouth.

"I finally know what I want to do with the money Willie left me."

"Great. Finish brushing your teeth and you can tell me." I winked.

"No. I want to tell you now," she mumbled.

I climbed out of bed, placed my hands on her hips, turned her around, and walked her to the bathroom sink.

"Spit," I said.

"Really? You always tell me to swallow." She smiled.

There was never a dull moment with her. "In this case, spit, Chloe."

After she brushed her teeth, I wiped her mouth with the towel and gave her a soft kiss.

"Okay, now you can tell me."

She rolled her eyes and climbed into bed. I climbed in next to her as she snuggled against me.

"I want to use the money to open up a homeless shelter in honor of him."

"What? Really?"

She lifted her head and sat up. "Yeah. Don't you like the idea?"

"I love the idea and I'll help you with everything. But what about your job at the gallery?"

"I'll still work at the gallery. We can hire someone to oversee it and enlist volunteers. I know for a fact that Ellery will help out. We can use the fifty thousand dollars to start it up and then you can ask your super rich corporate friends to make donations. In fact, we can hold a fundraiser."

"Sounds like you have it all figured out." I tapped her on the nose. "What took you so long to decide?"

"I actually decided it the day we were at the bank, but with Mercury being in retrograde, it just wasn't a good time to put the plan into action."

"I see, and why didn't you mention it to me then?"

"Because I didn't want to jinx it or get into a conversation and throw some bad mojo on it. Are you mad I didn't mention it?"

"No. I'm not mad. I just thought you told me everything."

"Honey, I do tell you everything." I placed my hand on his arm. "It was just an idea that had to wait. That's all."

"But that was an idea of importance. Something that meant a lot to you and you didn't share it with me."

"Aw, baby." I snuggled into him. I'm sorry. I didn't mean to hurt your feelings. I love you so much and I would never hurt you on purpose. You should know that. I just wanted to wait until the right time."

I felt his chest rise as he sighed. "I do know that and I love you too."

"I want you to be my partner in this. I want us to make decisions together, talk about ideas, and make magic happen for those less fortunate."

"Get up here and give me those gorgeous lips of yours."

Sitting up, I leaned over and he placed his hand on my cheek. Brushing his lips against mine, he spoke, "I'm so in love with you that I didn't think it was possible to love you anymore. But every day I spend with you, I find new ways to love you even more." He smiled.

"Sebastian." I traced his lips with my finger. "I love you so much."

"I know you do, baby. I know you do." He rolled me on my back and we made passionate love.

Chapter 42

Sebastian

"Well, what do you think, Sebastian?" Lenny asked.

"I think it's perfect," I spoke as I looked around.

"Excellent. So, you're interested in buying the property?"

"I am, but I'll let you know for sure in a few days."

Taking the small blue velvet box from my pocket, I opened it up and stared at the two-carat, princess cut, diamond-encased ring I had purchased. It felt right. The ring, the townhouse, everything. I had known that I was in love with her from our one night in London. We had our ups and downs in the beginning thanks to my stupidity. But now, we were the perfect couple. My love for her was so strong that marriage was the only thing I could see. I wanted to take our relationship to the next level; the ultimate commitment. When I thought of my future, the only thing I saw was her, us, together forever. She would like it here. We could make it our own and the memories that we'd create in this very home would be ones we'd hold on to forever.

I took in a deep breath as I closed the lid to the box and slipped it back into my pocket. She'd say yes. I knew she would. She loved me just as much and every day she made me feel it. She wasn't expecting this because we'd never talked about marriage. We were just happy to be with each other, and there wasn't one day I took her for granted. Every moment spent with her was just as magical as the moment before. She changed me. Something I never thought could happen.

The homeless shelter, Willie's Place, a shelter for the homeless, was now up and running. We held an elegant fundraiser at The Plaza Hotel where the elite of New York City were invited. I had pulled a few strings and made sure all the paperwork and licenses were expedited so we could get the shelter up and running as quickly as possible. We hired a director to oversee the day-to-day management of operations and hired a small staff to help. We enlisted the help of numerous volunteers including Chloe's mom and dad, and Sienna and Sam. Since the weekdays were busy for us between our jobs and everything else we had going on, the weekends were the days we spent most of our time there.

"Baby, come on. We're going to be late for dinner." I poked my head in the bathroom and stared at the beauty that stood before me.

"I'm coming. I'm just touching up my hair, considering someone messed it up just a few minutes ago." She smiled.

"Sorry. But you had me all horny and I couldn't help myself."

"I forgive you." She grabbed my chin and kissed me. "So where are we going anyway? You never said."

"It's a new restaurant that just opened."

"Cool. Where is it?"

"Not too far from here. You'll see when we get there."

Sliding into the limo next to her, my nerves were starting to get the best of me. I had no reason to be nervous, but it couldn't be helped. All the "what ifs" were running through my mind. What if she hated the townhouse? What if she hated the ring? What if she said no? What if she said she liked things the way they were? Don't get me wrong, I loved things the way they were, but I wanted and needed more.

"What are we doing here?" she asked as Eli pulled up to the curb on West 85th Street.

"I forgot to tell you that I had to stop by here and check something out for a client."

"Don't you have people that do that for you?"

"Yes. But this client is very special and I promised that I would do it myself."

"Oh cool. Can I come inside with you?" she asked with a grin.

"Of course you can."

Climbing out of the limo, I took her hand and helped her out. Walking through the wrought-iron gate, we climbed up the steps to the front door.

"The outside of this building is so beautiful," she spoke.

"Wait until you see the inside."

Unlocking the door, I opened it and led her inside.

"Wow. This place is a mess." She laughed.

"I know. But look at it beyond the mess."

"It's beautiful. So what do you have to check?" She turned and looked at me.

"It's over here in the living room."

Leading her into the living room by her hand, she looked at me with surprise.

"What is this?" she asked as she stared at the round, candlelit table draped with white linens, fine china, and a vase of gerbera daisies that was perfectly situated in front of the fireplace.

"This, my love, is where we're having dinner."

"Here? In an empty house?" She twisted her face.

"Yes. Here in this empty house."

"Sebastian, I love you to pieces, but I'm really confused right now."

I swallowed hard, trying to push down the lump in my throat. This was it. Hopefully, the night that would mark the beginning of us as an engaged couple and a life of happily ever after.

I took hold of both her hands and stared into her beautiful green eyes.

"Chloe, I never thought that I would ever be able to love someone. My heart was nothing but a rock solid stone. But then you came along and showed me that my life was lost without love. You hammered through all the stone until you reached my beating heart. A heart that wouldn't beat if you weren't in my life. You taught me things about life I never knew. You helped me to embrace my past and you took away the anger and bitterness that resided inside me for so many years."

She stood there and listened to me as a tear fell from her eye. Taking my thumb and bringing it to her face, I gently wiped it away.

"You turned my dark and stormy life into one that is full of brightness and purpose. We were meant to meet that night at the bar in London, just like we were meant to meet again here in New York. It was all in the timing, baby. The universe had it planned out perfectly for us. I was brought into this world to love you."

I reached in my pocket and pulled out the box, got down on one knee while I held her hand, and proposed to her.

"Chloe, I want nothing more in this life than for you to become my wife." I flipped the lid open and revealed the ring. "Will you marry me?"

She cupped her right hand over her mouth as she stared into my eyes.

"Oh my God, Sebastian. Yes! Yes! Yes! I will marry you!"

I let out a sigh of relief as I took the ring from the box and placed it on her finger.

"Holy shit, that's huge." She smiled as she held her hand out in front of her.

"Do you like it?"

"I love it. I adore it and I love you, Sebastian Bennett," she spoke as the back of her hand ran down my cheek.

Standing up, I wrapped my arms around her and gently kissed her lips.

"I love you too. More than you'll ever know."

"I have a pretty good idea how much." She grinned as another tear fell from her eye.

"No tears." I wiped it away.

"They're happy tears. I can't believe you did all this. I can't believe we're engaged! But I do have one tiny little question."

"What's your question, baby?"

"What's up with the house?"

I let out a chuckle. "Take a look around, Chloe, because I want us to make this our home."

"Shut up!" she exclaimed. "Are you serious?"

"Very serious." I smiled.

"I love it and it needs a lot of work." She looked around.

"I know it does and me and you are going to do it together."

"Huh?" She bit down on her bottom lip.

"We're going to fix this place up together, and I'm going to teach you a few things in the carpentry world. We're going to knock out walls together, saw wood together, and hammer nails. I'm going to go back to a time when I enjoyed doing those things, before I started Bennett Enterprises."

"Wow. I think I just fell in love with you all over again."

"Keep remembering that while we're working on the house." I smiled.

"Can we have a lot of sex while we're knocking out walls and being all sweaty?" she asked with a wide grin.

"We can have all the sex you want." I kissed her. "Now, if you'll take a seat at the table, dinner will be served in a moment."

I pulled out my phone and alerted the caterers to bring in the food. As dinner was being served, Chloe couldn't stop looking at her ring.

"This ring is so beautiful, Sebastian. I love the cut of the diamond. It's one of my favorites."

"I thought the cut was fitting since it was for a princess." The corners of my mouth curved upwards.

"Stop." She looked up at the ceiling. "The tears are coming again."

I grabbed her hand from across the table and brought her ring up to my lips.

"When are we going to make the announcement?" I asked.

"I can hardly contain myself right now. But we should wait at least until tomorrow. What do you think about having my parents, Sam, and Sienna over for dinner tomorrow night and we'll tell them all at once?"

"I love the idea. I'll let Karina know and have her make something special."

"Great. Let me send a group message now. But I have to do it in a way where they won't suspect. I'll just tell them that we need to discuss something about the shelter."

****

Chloe

Opening my eyes, I held out my hand and looked at my ring. I was still in shock that Sebastian asked me to marry him since I thought that it would be years before he was ready. Even if it took that long, I was willing to wait because he was more than worth it.

"It still smells like sex in here," Sebastian mumbled as he kissed my head.

"Well, considering we had sex when we came home last night and then again just a couple of hours ago, I would say it would."

"Sorry, but I woke up and I was hard. I couldn't let that go to waste."

I smiled as I sat up and kissed him. "I'm not complaining. Trust me. We have to get up now. The alarm will be going off in about five minutes."

"Do we have to?" He closed his eyes.

"Yes." I softly stroked his chest.

After showering together and having sex again, we got dressed and headed to the kitchen for breakfast.

"Good morning, Karina." I smiled.

"Good morning, Chloe. Mr. Bennett," she spoke as she handed us some coffee.

"Morning, Karina. We're having dinner guests tonight, so can you cook something nice?"

"What would you like, sir?" she asked.

"Chloe?" Sebastian looked at me.

"I don't know. Remember, my parents are vegetarians."

"How about filet for us, Sam, and Sienna, and a vegetarian dish for your parents?"

"Sounds good to me." I smiled.

"You know, how come your parents don't mind that you eat meat?"

"I'm my own person and I make my own decisions. They never forced it on me. Although growing up, all I ate was vegetarian meals that she cooked, but then headed to nearest burger place and ate the biggest burger I could get my hands on."

He chuckled. "You can prepare something vegetarian for Chloe's parents?" he asked Karina.

"Yes, Mr. Bennett. I can do that."

"Thank you, Karina."

As I took a sip of my coffee, I looked at Karina, who was preparing omelets for us.

"You can call him Sebastian." I smiled.

"Excuse me?" Sebastian raised his brow.

"What?" I raised my brow back. "There's no need to be so formal. We're adults, not children. Just because she works for you doesn't mean she has to call you Mr. Bennett. She's not on any different level than you are. We're all the same human beings and should be treated as such. If she's going to call you Mr. Bennett all the time, then you should be calling her Miss Young."

"Okay, okay." He grabbed my chin. "Can you please just be quiet? No more Mr. Bennett, Karina. From now on, you are to refer to me as Sebastian." He went and took a seat at the table.

"Yes, sir."

"No 'sir,' Karina." I winked. "Just Sebastian."

Chapter 43

Chloe

I finally finished hanging the last of Caden's newest artwork and took a step back. He was such a good artist and one that was on the rise, thanks to us. His artwork was selling faster than he could paint it. Just as I was walking into my office, I heard Connor and Ellery coming up the stairs.

"Hello, Chloe," Connor spoke.

"Hey, Connor. Ellery. What brings you by?"

"We just wanted to let you know that we're heading to California to check on things at the other gallery and we'll be out there for a couple of weeks at the beach house."

"Great. Have fun. Enjoy that warm Cali sun." I smiled.

As they followed me into my office, Ellery spoke, "You seem different."

"I do?"

"Yes. You're glowing. You know we woman can tell when something wonderful happened. Are you pregnant?" she asked with a wide grin.

I was dying. I needed to tell someone about our engagement and I knew Connor and Ellery would keep it to themselves.

"No. I'm not pregnant. But," I reached into my purse and put on my ring, "Sebastian asked me to marry him!" I exclaimed in a soft voice.

Ellery cupped her hands over her mouth. "Oh my God. That's wonderful."

"Congratulations, Chloe. That makes me very happy," Connor spoke.

"You and me both. He proposed last night in the townhouse that he's buying for us."

"Oh. So you're moving again?" He laughed.

"Yeah. But it won't be for a while. The house needs some fixing up and Sebastian said that the two of us are doing it together."

Connor frowned as he looked at me. "You mean you'll plan it out and hire a company to renovate it for you."

"No. We're doing the work ourselves." I grinned.

"But why?" he asked with a perplexed look.

"I think it's wonderful that Sebastian wants to the do the work himself," Ellery chimed in as she lightly smacked Connor on his chest.

"You know he fixed up houses himself before he started his company," I spoke.

"Well, yes, but I thought now he wouldn't want to do that anymore," Connor frowned again.

"He's very excited about it."

"Well, if you need Connor's help, just call. I'm sure he wouldn't mind getting his hands dirty to help some friends." Ellery grinned. "Right, Connor?"

"Of course."

Ellery walked over and gave me a hug. "We have a flight to catch. Congratulations to you and Sebastian. That ring is gorgeous."

"Thank you, Ellery. Have a safe flight."

As Ellery was walking out the door, Connor gave me a hug and whispered in my ear, "Do me a favor and don't call. If you need any help at all, I can arrange it for you."

I laughed. "Don't worry. I wasn't planning on it."

****

"You almost ready, babe?" Sebastian shouted from the closet. "They're going to be here in a few minutes. Well, make that now because I just heard the doorbell."

"You go. I'll be there in a few."

I took off my ring and placed it in my pocket. Checking myself one last time in the mirror, I headed towards the living room where my mom and dad had just sat down.

"Where's Chloe?" my dad asked.

"She's in the bathroom."

"Aw, did you two just finish having sex?" my mom spoke.

"We sure did." I walked in with a smile and gave them each a hug, then took Arlo from her arms.

I heard Sebastian mumble under his breath as he walked over to the bar with my dad for a drink. The doorbell rang again and Karina answered it, letting in Sienna and Sam.

"Hello, darling." Sienna smiled as she hugged me. "Oh, hello there, you sweet little man."

"Hi. You're late. Were you two having sex?" I grinned.

"We sure were, beautiful," Sam answered as he hugged me and then kissed Arlo on the head.

I could hear Sebastian sigh all the way across the room and I silently giggled.

"Dinner will be ready in a few minutes, so why don't we go into the dining room and sit down?"

Setting Arlo down in his bouncy seat, I took my seat next to Sebastian and discreetly slipped on my ring. Taking hold of my hand from under the table, he lightly gave it a squeeze.

"So what's going on with the shelter?" my mom asked.

"Nothing. The shelter is doing really well," I replied. "There's something else I need to tell you."

"OH MY GOD, YOU'RE PREGNANT!" Sienna shouted from across the table.

I held up my left hand. "Sebastian and I are getting married!" I exclaimed.

"Holy shit, look at that ring!" Sienna squealed. "Congratulations!"

"Oh, sweetheart, congratulations," my mom spoke as she wiped her eye.

"Wow. My daughter is getting married." My dad stood up from his chair.

"Way to go, you two." Sam smiled.

Sebastian and I got up from our seats and made our rounds of hugs.

"So are you pregnant?" Sienna asked.

"No. I'm not pregnant. Just engaged."

"Have you set a date yet?" my mom asked.

"No. It just happened last night. We wanted you to be the first to know." There was no way I was telling them that I already told Connor and Ellery.

"There's something else," Sebastian spoke. "I am purchasing a townhouse on West 85th Street for the two of us."

"An engagement and a new house. How exciting." My mom grinned. "I'm so happy for the both of you." She hugged us again.

It was a wonderful evening spent with family. We drank, laughed, and had great conversations. Every time I looked at Sebastian, his face displayed a mouthwatering smile. He fit in with us perfectly and he knew it.

"Well, we better get going and get Arlo home to bed," my mom spoke.

"Yeah. I'm sure the two of them want to go have sex again to celebrate this night." My dad winked.

"We sure do!" I grinned as I patted Sebastian's ass.

"Chloe!" He shot me a look.

"Get used to it, babe. You're part of this sex-crazed family now." I smiled.

He slowly shook his head as we walked to the door and hugged each of them goodbye. After brushing my teeth, I climbed into bed and blew in Sebastian's face.

"I'm all fresh for you now and my mouth isn't the only thing." I smiled.

He let out a growl as he pulled me on top of him. "Good to know because your mouth won't be the only thing I'll be spending a lot of time on."

"Bring it on, fiancé." I brushed my lips against his.

Chapter 44

Sebastian

"We really should set a date," I spoke as she lay wrapped tightly in my arms.

"It should definitely be in the summer or early fall." Her fingers ran up and down my arm.

"Whenever you want, but I don't want to wait too long. I want you as Mrs. Chloe Bennett as soon as possible."

"I like the sound of that. We need to decide where we're going to get married."

"I know where we're going on our honeymoon," I spoke.

"You do?"

"Yep."

"Where?"

"We will be spending our honeymoon in London, at the same hotel where we first met. The place that led us to where we are today."

"You mean where we had sex, because we technically didn't meet. I mean, we didn't know each other's names, so we really never officially met. We just had sex and more sex without knowing each other. We were still strangers when we saw each other at the gallery."

"Chloe, shush." I smiled as I kissed her head. "Wait a minute. When we saw each other at the gallery, Connor introduced us, so we weren't strangers."

"We were when I saw you and ran to the bathroom so you didn't see me. And also that time outside the restaurant when you were talking to Damien."

"What are you talking about?"

"Shit." She sat up and bit down on her bottom lip.

"Shit what? Are you telling me that you saw me before I saw you again at the gallery and you didn't say something to me?" I asked with irritation.

"Uh huh?"

"Oh my God. I can't believe you would do that. Especially since we slept together."

"I'm sorry." She pouted. "I thought about you every single day after that night. When I woke up, you were gone and it took me a long time to try to forget you. When I saw you, I freaked out. Like, I put on sunglasses at night and pulled the hood over my head."

"Jesus, Chloe. I remember that night. That was you?"

"Yeah."

"I remember looking at you and thinking you were strange."

She shrugged. "Nothing new there. After that night in London, I was pretty sure I fell in love with you, even though I didn't know you. I felt this connection that I had never felt before. A pull towards a total stranger. Then all of a sudden, there you were; here in New York City. The same city that I just moved back to. God, seeing you again, Sebastian, took me back to that night and I got scared. Scared that if you saw me again, you wouldn't even remember or just totally blow me off, and I wasn't sure if I could handle the rejection."

"Baby." I placed my hand on her cheek. "I want to show you something." I reached for my phone and pulled up the picture of her I took in London.

Her brow raised. "You took this of me while I was sleeping?"

"Yeah. I took it before I left."

"Why?"

"Because, baby, like you, I felt something that I had never felt before. I wanted something to always remember that night and I looked at that picture every single day after. You, Chloe, were on my mind at all times. So if you would have approached me that night outside the restaurant, I would have welcomed you with open arms and brought you back here for another night of amazing sex." I smiled.

"Wow. I'm sorry."

I swept my hand across her cheek and pushed her hair behind her ear. "Maybe the time wasn't right yet for us to reconnect that night."

327

A beautiful smile crossed her lips. "I guess it wasn't."

"But wait a minute." I shook my head. "After that night we officially met at the gallery, you ran from me and pretended you didn't know me. Why?"

"Because." She looked down. "I was honestly afraid of what you thought about me because of what happened in London and I really liked you, even though I didn't know you, and it bothered me that maybe you thought I was nothing but some sex-crazed girl."

"But you are." I grinned.

"Sebastian." She lightly smacked my chest.

"Come here." I pulled her into me and kissed the top of her head. "It doesn't matter, baby. All that matters is that we're here now, we're getting married, and starting a beautiful future together. I love you."

"I love you too. Can we have makeup sex now?"

"Makeup sex? We didn't have a fight."

She lifted her head. "I sensed a little hostility and anger in your voice, so technically, you were mad at me. Because if you weren't, you wouldn't have used the tone you did."

Placing my finger over her lips, I spoke, "Shush. We're going to have makeup sex now and I don't want you telling your parents about it."

"Aw, you're no fun." She grinned.

This crazy girl, who I loved more than life itself, made me the happiest man in the world. She loved me for who I was and I loved her just as much for who she was. Yes, she tried my patience at times, but life without her would be boring and predictable. Two things I would never experience again with her by my side. She was the girl who stole my heart, all thanks to that One Night in London. A night that was planned out all along by a thing we called fate.

About The Author

Sandi Lynn is a New York Times, USA Today and Wall Street Journal bestselling author who spends all of her days writing. She published her first novel, Forever Black, in February 2013 and hasn't stopped writing since. Her addictions are shopping, going to the gym, romance novels, coffee, chocolate, margaritas, and giving readers an escape to another world.

Please come connect with her at:

www.facebook.com/Sandi.Lynn.Author

www.twitter.com/SandilynnWriter

www.authorsandilynn.com

www.pinterest.com/sandilynnWriter

www.instagram.com/sandilynnauthor

https://www.goodreads.com/author/show/6089757.Sandi_Lynn

CPSIA information can be obtained
at www.ICGtesting.com
Printed in the USA
LVOW04s0131070316

478028LV00030B/738/P